IS THE DEVIL A GENTLEMAN?

AND OTHER SATANIC STORIES

BY

VARIOUS AUTHORS

British Library Cataloguing-in-Publication Data
A catalogue record for this book is available from the
British Library

CONTENTS

IS THE DEVIL A GENTLEMAN?...................5

MONSIEUR SEEKS A WIFE.........................52

THE DREAM CIRCEAN.............................103

THE PRIMATE OF THE ROSE 133

WITCHES' HOLLOW................................160

SEABURY QUINN....................................187

MARGARET IRWIN..................................188

ALEISTER CROWLEY...............................189

M. P. SHIEL...190

H. P. LOVECRAFT..................................191

IS THE DEVIL A GENTLEMAN?

SEABURY QUINN

It had been a day of strange weather, a day the calendar declared to be late April and the thermometer proclaimed to be March or November. From dawn till early dark the rain had spattered down, chill, persistent, deceptive, making it feel many degrees colder than it really was, but just at sunset it had cleared and a sort of angry yellow half-light had spilled from a sky of streaky black against a bank of blood-red clouds. Now, while the dying wind was groping with chill-stiffened fingers at the window-casings, a fire blazed on the study hearth, its comforting rose glow a gleaming island in the gathering shadows, its reflection daubing ever-changing pattern on the walls and tightly-drawn curtains.

'On such a night,' the Bishop quoted inexactly as he helped himself to brandy, 'mine enemy s dog, though he had bit me, I would not turn away from my door.'

Dr. Bentley, rector of St. Chrysostom's, dropped a second lump of sugar in his coffee and said nothing. He knew the Bishop, and had known him since their student days. When he quoted Shakespeare he was really searching through the lumber rooms of memory for a story, and there were few who had a better store of anecdotes than the Right Reverend Richard Chauncev, missionary, soldier, preacher and ecclesiastical executive, worldly man of God and godly man of the world. He'd looked forward to Dick's coming down for confirmation, and had made a point of asking Kitteringson in to dinner. Kitteringson was all right, of course; good, earnest worker, a good preacher and a good churchman, but a trifle too—how should he put it?—too dogmatic. If you couldn't find it in the writings of the Fathers of the Church or the Thirty-nine Articles he was against a proposition, whatever it might be. A session with the Bishop would be good for him.

'Good stuff in the lad,' thought Dr. Bentley as he studied his junior covetly. A rather strong, intelligent face he had, but marked by asceticism, the face of one who might be either an unyielding martyr or a merciless inquisitor. Now he was leaning forward almost eagerly, and the firelight did things to his earnest face-made it look like one of those old medieval monks in the old masters' paintings.

'I've been wondering all day, sir,' he told Bishop Chauncey, 'what you meant when you told the confirmation class they should use common sense about religious prejudices. Surely, there may be no compromise with evil—'

'I shouldn't care to lay that down as a precept,' the Bishop answered with a low chuckle. 'We're told the Devil can quote Scripture for his purposes; why shouldn't Christians make use of the powers of darkness in a proper case?'

Young Dr. Kitteringson was aghast. 'Make use of Satan?' he faltered. 'Have dealings with the arch-fiend—'

'Precisely, son. Shakespeare might have been more truthful than poetical when he declared the Prince of Darkness is a gentleman.'

'I can't conceive of such a thing!' the younger man retorted. 'All our experiences tell us—'

'All?' cut in Bishop Chauncey softly, and the young rector fell hesitant before the level irony of his gaze. 'How old are you, son?'

'Thirty-two, sir, but I've read the writings of the Fathers of the Early Church, and one and all they tell us mat to compromise with evil is a sin against—' He stopped, a little abashed at the look of tolerant amusement on his senior's face, then: 'Can you name even one case when compromise with evil didn't end disastrously for all concerned, sir?' he challenged.

'Yes, I think I can,' the Bishop passed the brandy sniffer back and forth beneath his nostrils, inhaled the bouquet of the old cognac appreciatively, then took a delicate, approving sip. 'I think I can, son. Like you, I have to call upon my reading to sustain me, but unlike you I can't claim ecclesiastical authority for my writers. One of them, indeed, was an ancestor of mine, a great-grandfather several times removed.'

The gloom that waited just beyond the moving edge of firelight seemed flowing forward, like a slowly rising, stagnant tide, and a blazing ember falling to the layer of sand beneath the burning logs sent a sudden shaft of light across the intervening shade, casting a quick shadow of the Bishop on the farther wall. An odd shadow it was, not like the rubicund, grey-haired churchman, but queerly elongated and distorted, so that it appeared to be the shade of a lean man with gaunt and predatory features, muffled in a cloak and leaning forward at the shoulders, like one intent—almost in the act of pouncing.

Kundre Maltby (said the Bishop, drawing thoughtfully at his cigar so its recurrent glow etched his face in alternate red highlight and black shadow) was a confessed witch, and witches, as you know, are those who have made solemn compact with the Evil One.

She was a Swedish girl—at least she claimed that she was Swedish—whom Captain Pelatiah Maltby had found somewhere in his travels, married, and brought back to Danby by Salem. Who she really was nobody knew.

Captain Maltby's ship, the *Bountiful Adventure*, came on

her Easter Monday morning, clinging to a hatch-grating some twenty miles or so off the Madeira coast. He'd cleared from Funchal the night before, swearing that he'd never make the port again, for the Portuguese had celebrated Easter with an *auto da fé* at which a hundred condemned witches had been burned, and the sight of the poor wretches' sufferings sickened him. When he asked the castaway her name she told him it was Kundre, and said her ship had been the *Blenkinge* of Stockholm, wrecked three days before.

Maltby marvelled at this information, for he had been in the Madeiras for a whole week, and there had been no storm, not even a light squall. But there the girl was, lashed to the floating hatch-top, virtually nude and all but dead with thirst and starvation. Moreover, she had very winning ways and more than a fair share of beauty, so Captain Maltby asked no further questions, but put in at New York and married her before he brought the *Bountiful Adventure* up the coast to Danby.

Their life together seems to have been ideal, possibly idyllic. He was a raw-boned, tough-thewed son of New England, hard as flint outside and practical as the multiplication tables within. But it was from such ancestry that Whittier and Holmes and Bryant and Longfellow sprang, and probably beneath his workaday exterior Pelatiah Maltby had a poet's soul. They had twin children, a boy and a girl. At Pelatiah s insistence the girl was named for her mother, but Kundre chose the name of Micah for the boy, for in the whole Scripture she liked best that Prophet's question, 'What doth the Lord require of thee, but to do justly, and to love mercy, and to walk humbly with thy God?'

She took to transplantation like a hardy flower, and grew and flourished on New England soil. From all accounts she must have been a beauty in a heavy Nordic way, a true woman of the sea. Full six feet tall she was, and strong as any man, yet with all the gracious curves of womanhood. Her hair, they say, was golden. Not merely yellow, but that metallic shade of gold which, catching glints of outside light, seems to hold a light of its own. And her skin was white as sea-foam, and her eyes the bright blue-green of the ice of the fjords, and her lips were red as sunset on the ocean when a storm has blown itself away.

Prosperity came with her, too. The winds were always favourable to Captain Maltby's ship. He made the longest voyages in the shortest time. When other ships were set upon by tempests and battered till they were mere hulks he came safely through the raving storms or missed them altogether, and his enterprises always prospered. Foreign traders sold him goods at laughably low prices, or bought the cargoes that he brought at prices that astonished him.

He brought back treasures from the far corners of the

earth, silks from Cathay and Nippon, carved coral from the South Sea Isles, pearls from Java, diamonds from Africa, a comb of solid beaten gold from India—and the golden comb seemed pallid when she drew it through the golden spate of her loosed golden hair.

The neighbours were first amazed, then wondering, finally suspicious. Experience had taught them Providence dealt even-handedly with men and balanced its smiles with its frowns. Yet Pelatiah Maltby always won, He never had to drain a cup of vinegar to compensate him for the many heady cups of the wine of success he quaffed.

It was Captain Joel Newton who brought matters to a head. He and Captain Maltby had been rivals many years. His pew was just across the aisle from Maltby's in the meeting house, his wife sat where she could not help but see the worldly gewgaws Maltby lavished on Kundre, and Abigail Newton's tongue had an edge like that of a new-filed adze, and her jealousy the bitter bite of acid. Joel Newton heard himself compared to Pelatiah Maltby, with small advantage, every Lord's Day after service, and, driven by the lash of a shrew's tongue, he determined to find the key to Maltby's constant success, and set himself deliberately to trail the *Bountiful Adventure* from one port to another.

Not that it helped him. The *Bountiful Adventure* outsailed him every trip, and when he came into a foreign berth he found that Maltby had been there before him, secured what trade there was, and sailed away.

They came face to face at last at Tamatave in Madagascar. Maltby had traded rum and salted fish and tobacco for a holdful of rich native silver, and the local traders had no thought of laying in new stocks for months. Newton's ship was loaded to capacity with just the wares that Maltby had disposed of so profitably, there was no market for his cargo, his food was running tow, and ruin stared him in the face.

Both had taken more of the French wines the inn purveyed than was their custom. Maltby was flushed with success, Newton bitter with the mordancy of disappointment. 'Had I a witch-woman for wife I'd always fare well, too,' he told his rival.

'How quotha?' Maltby asked. 'What meanest, knave? My Kundre is the fairest, sweetest bloom—'

'As ever sank its taproots deep in hell,' his rival finished for him, 'Oh, don't 'ee think to fool us, Neighbour Maltby! We know what 'tis that always sends the fair winds at thy tail when others lie becalmed. We know what 'tis that makes the heathen take thy wares at such great prices, and pay thee ten times what thou'd hoped to get. Aye, and we know whence comes thy witch-mate, too—how the Papishers had burned a drove of warlocks in the Madeiras the day before ye found her floating in the ocean. She said her vessel had been wrecked three days before, but had there been a storm? Thou knowest well there had not. Did'st offer her free passage back to the island, and did she take thy offer kindly?'

Now this was a poser, for Pelatiah had offered to set Kundre on shore at Funchal when he rescued her, and she had refused tearfully, and begged him to hold to his course.

'And why?' asked Captain Newton as he warmed to his task of denunciation. 'I'll tell 'ee why, my fine bucko— because she was a cursed witch who'd slipped between the Papists' fingers and made use of thee to ferry her to safety. Thinkest thou she loves thee? Faugh! While thou'rt away she wantons it with every man 'twixt Danby and old Salem Town———'

'Thou liar!' The scandalous words were like to have been Joel's last, for Pelatiah drew his hanger and made for him with intent to stab the slander down his throat with cold steel, but Joel was just a thought too quick.

Before his rival reached him he jerked a pistol from his waistband and let fly, striking Captain Maltby fairly in the chest. Afterwards he boasted that it was a silver bullet he had used, since, as everybody knew, witches, warlocks and were-beasts were impervious to lead, but vulnerable to silver missiles.

However that might be Captain Maltby halted in mid-stride, and his hanger fell with a clatter from his unnerved hand. He hiccoughed once and tried to draw a breath that stopped before he had it in, sagged at the knees, fell on his side and died. But with that last unfinished breath they say he whispered, 'Kundre dearest, they have done for me and will for thee if so be that they can. God have thee in His keeping—'

Maltby, of course, was a Protestant, and the only Christian cemetery in the town was Catholic. It was not possible a heretic should lie in consecrated ground, but the missionary priest took counsel with the rabbi of the little Jewish congregation and arranged to buy a grave-site in the Hebrew burying ground.

There was no ordained minister of his faith to do the final service for Maltby, so the priest and rabbi stood beside his grave, and one said Christian prayers in Latin, and the other Jewish prayers in Hebrew, while the grim-faced sailors from New England stood by and marvelled at this show of charity in those they had been taught to hate, and responded with tear-choked 'A-mens' when prayers were done and time had come to heap the earth upon the body sewn in sailcloth in lieu of a coffin.

It was a Wednesday in mid-April when the killing took place, and Kundre, so the story goes, was sitting beside the brooklet that ran through her back-lot. The weather was unseasonably warm, and her children waded in the stream and searched for buds of ground-rose while she sunned and bleached the hair that was her greatest pride—or vanity, according to the neighbours' wives. Suddenly she raised her head like one who listens to a hail from far away, shook back her clouding hair and cupped one hand to her ear to sit there statue-still for a long moment. Then, with a cry that seemed to be the echo of her riven heart-strings' breaking, she called out, 'Pelatiah! Oh beloved!' and fell forward on her face beside the brooklet, lying with her arms outstretched before her like a diver's when he strikes the water, while her great, heroically-formed body twitched and jerked, and little, dreadful moans came bubbling from her lips, like blood that wells and bubbles from a mortal wound.

Presently she rose and dried her eyes and went into the house where she laid away her gown of crisp blue linen and put on widow's weeds before she sought Ezekiel Martin the stone-mason and ordered him to cut and set a gravestone in the village churchyard. You could see that tombstone now if you should go to Danby burying ground. It reads:

Sacred to the memory of
PELATIAH MALTBY
Chriſtian man & feacaptain
Moſt foully done to death by jealouſie
at Tamatave in Madagaſcie

Now, you'll allow it would be cause for comment, even in these days when extrasensory perceptions are taken as more or less established facts, for a woman to become aware of her husband's death half-way round the world from her at the very moment of its happening. The circumstances caused comment in mid-seventeenth century New England, too, but not at all of the same kind. Everybody dreaded sorcery and witchcraft then, and in every unexplained occurrence men saw Satan's ungloved hand. So when Kundre went forth in her mourning clothes, sorrowing dry-eyed at the empty grave where she had placed the tombstone, neighbours looked at her from beneath lowered lids, and when she went to divine service at the meeting house the tithing man went past her hurriedly, and hardly paused to hold the alms basin before her, though he knew it would be heavier by a gold piece minted with the symbol of King Charles' majesty when he withdrew it.

In August came the *Bountiful Adventure* with her ensign flying at half-mast, and Captain Maltby's death was confirmed by the sorrowing seamen.

But what became of Captain Joel Newton and his ship the *Crystal Wave* nobody ever knew. He had set sail from Tamatava the same day he shot Maltby, for everyone agreed he had provoked the quarrel, and the commandant of the garrison threatened his arrest unless he drew his anchor from the harbour-mud at once. The rest was silence. Neither stick nor spar nor broken bit of wreckage ever washed ashore to show the *Crystal Wave's* fate, or that of Captain Joel Newton and the twenty seamen of his crew.

Voyages of a year or even two years were the rule those days, and it was not until King Charles had been beheaded and the Lord Protector proclaimed that Abigail Newton descended from the 'widow's watch' that topped her square-roofed house beside the harbour and changed her home-spun gown of blue for one of black linsey woolsey, then sent for Zeke Martin the mason to cut and set a stone in Danby churchyard.

The twenty widows of the *Crystal Wave's* crew also went in mourning, and bewailed their joint and several losses piteously. When they passed Kundre in the street they looked away, but when she'd gotten safely past they spit upon the ground and muttered 'witch!' and 'Devil's-hag!'

Kundre was a Swedish woman, and though the good folk of Danby had small use for King James's politics and even less for his religion, they were with him to a man in his views on witchcraft. Moreover, they recalled how Scandinavian witches had raised storms and tempests to prevent the Princess Anne from reaching Scotland where her marriage to King James was to be solemnized, and some of the more learned in the village knew the legends of *Sangreal* and remembered that the temptress who all but kept the Holy Grail from Parsifal was named Kundry. There seemed little difference between her name and Kundre's. Kundry of the legend was a witch damned past redemption, might not Kundre—the strange outland woman who knew of her husband's death four months before the news came home—also be a potent witch?

It seemed entirely possible and even probable, and when the widowed Abigail met widowed Kundre in the village street and taxed her with destroying both the *Crystal Wave's* master and crew by witchcraft, something happened to confirm the worst suspicions.

'Thou art a wicked, Devil-vowed and wanton witch!' said Abigail in hearing of at least three neighbour women. 'By thy vile arts thou raised a monstrous storm and sank the *Crystal Wave* and all her people in the ocean.'

Kundre looked at her, and in her ice-blue eyes there seemed to kindle a slow light like that which the aurora borealis makes on winter nights. 'Thy tongue is dipped in venom like a serpent's, Goody Newton,' she replied in the deep voice which was her Nordic heritage. 'It never wags except to hurt thy neighbours, so 'twere best thou never used it hereafter.'

Whether from the look in Kundre's eyes, or from astonishment that anyone should dare to tell her to keep still we do not know, but it was amply attested that Abigail for once had no reply to make, and we find in the old town records of Danby that on the evening after this encounter she lost her power of speech completely. More, she lost the use of her tongue, for it swelled and swelled until she could not keep it in her mouth, and she could take no nourishment but liquids, and those with greatest difficulty.

In the light of present-day medical knowledge it would not be too difficult to attribute her misfortune to that rare condition known as macroglossia or hypertrophy of the tongue, which doctors tell us is due to engorgement and dilation of the lymph channels. Most of us who have served in hospitals have seen such cases, where the swollen tongue hangs from the mouth and gives the patient a peculiarly idiotic look. But medicine was far from an exact science those days, and besides there was the testimony of the women who had seen the curse of silence laid on Abigail. Three hours after sunset Kundre was 'spoken against' as a witch and duly lodged in Danby jail.

By the common law of England torture was forbidden to force a prisoner to accuse himself, but by the witchcraft statutes of King James certain "tests" which differed from torture neither in degree nor kind were permitted. One of these was known as "swimming," for it was believed a witch's body was so buoyed up with evil that it could not sink in water.

Accordingly, upon the second day of her confinement Kundre was brought out to be "swum." Stripped to her shift they led her from the jail to the horse-pond which served the village as reservoir and ornamental lake at once, forced her to sit cross-legged on the ground and tied her right thumb to her left great toe, her right great toe to her left thumb with heavy linen thread which had been waxed for greater strength, and to make it cut more deeply in the tender flesh. Then over her they dropped a linen bed-sheet, tumbled her all helpless as she was upon her side and tied the sheets loose ends together, exactly as a modern housewife makes a laundry bundle ready. A rope was fastened to the knotted sheet and willing hands laid hold on it and dragged it out into the water.

Now here we have a choice between the natural and the supernatural. We have all seen the properties of wet cloth to retain the air and resist water. The device known as water wings with which so many children learn to swim is simply a cloth bladder wet before inflation, and as long as outside pressure is evenly applied it will support surprisingly large weights in calm water.

Perhaps it was as natural a phenomenon as this that kept the accused woman afloat on the calm surface of the village horse-pond. Perhaps, again, it was something more sinister. At any rate, the sheeted bundle bobbed and floated on the quiet surface of the pool as easily as if it had been filled with cork, and a great shout went up from the spectators 'She swims! She swims; it is the judgement of just Heaven; she is a proven witch!'

Her trial lasted a full day, and people came from miles about to hear the evidence poured on her. Ezekiel Martin the stonemason told how she came to him and ordered him to cut the tombstone for a man whose limbs were scarcely stiff in death, though none could know that he had died until his ship came a full four months later.

There was no dearth of testimony concerning the fine winds and weather that had been her husband's portion since he married her, or concerning the storms that had plagued his rivals.

Abigail Newton stood up in court that all might see her swollen tongue, and though she could not speak, she went through an elaborate dumb-show of the way the curse had been laid on her. Less reticent, Flee-from-the-Wrath-to-Come Epsworth, Rebecca Norris and Susan Clayton told under oath how they had seen and heard Kundre strike Abigail with speechlessness.

A tithe of such evidence would have been enough to hang her, and the jury took but fifteen minutes to deliberate upon their verdict, which, of course, was guilty.

Asked what she had to say in her defence before the court

pronounced sentence, she made a seemly curtsey to the judge and answered without hesitation ' 'Tis true I am a witch as ye have charged me. Long years agone, my sire and dam made compact with the Prince of Evil and bound me by their covenant, but never have I used my power to hurt a living creature, brute or human. That I should wish my man to prosper was but natural. Thus far I used my power over wind and tides, but no farther. Whether Heaven punished Goodman Newton for the foul murder that he did on my poor man I cannot say. I know naught of the matter, nor did I lift a finger to bring Heaven's retribution on him. "Vengeance is mine, I will repay," saith the Lord.

'As for the swollen tongue of von shrew, belike it is the malice of her black and jealous heart that bloats it. As to that I cannot answer; but hark ye, neighbours, if I had the power to release her I'd not use it. The town is better for her silence, as I wis ye all agree.'

With that she made another curtsey to the judge and stood there silent, waiting sentence: 'Since, therefore, Goodwife Kundre Maltby hath by her own confession admitted she was justly tried and convicted, so let her on account of her bond with the Devil and on account of the witchcraft she hath practised, be hanged by the neck until she be dead.'

The usual formula in hanging cases was for the court to add, 'and may God have mercy on thy soul,' but such a sentiment seemed obviously out of place here, and the judge forbore to express it.

They carried out the sentence next day, and a mighty crowd was gathered for the spectacle. The members of the trained band were much put to it to control the rabble when the hangman drove his cart beneath the gallows tree and made the hemp fast to her neck.

She wore her widow's weeds to execution, and round her neck was clasped a slender chain of some base metal with a flat pendant like a coin hung from it. It was the only ornament she'd had when Pelatiah found her floating on the grating, and she had laid it by when they were married. Now, through a whim, perhaps, she chose to wear it at her death.

They'd let her children visit her in jail the night before, and she had sent the girl back for the bauble. 'Look well on it, my sweet,' she told the child when it was clasped about her neck. 'The time may come when thou'lt have need of it, and if it comes thou shalt not cry for it in vain.'

As the hangman bound her elbows to her sides before he slipped the noose beneath her chin she begged him, 'Leave the worthless chain in place when thy grim task is done, good Peter Grimes. In my left shoe thoult find a golden sovereign hidden to repay thee for thy work. Take it and welcome, but if thou take'st the chain and pendant from me—a witch's curse shall be on thee.'

Peter Grimes was a poor man, and the clothes a felon stood in when he died were part of his perquisites, but he had no stomach for a witch's curse, so when he found the gold piece in her shoe as she had promised he took it and was well pleased to leave the worthless chain in place.

She did not die easily, from all accounts. Her splendid body was too powerful, the tide of life ran too strong in her, so she dangled, quivering and writhing in the air a full five minutes. Then Peter Grimes, perhaps in charity, perhaps because he wished to have the business over with and go home to his breakfast, seized her by the legs and dragged until the double burden of his weight and hers proved too much for her spinal column, and with a snapping like the cracking of a fire-dried stick her neck broke and her struggles ended.

They raised the stone that she had set above her husband's empty grave, scooped out a shallow opening beneath it and dropped her in, coffinless and without proper graveclothes. So, as the neighbours sagely said, she had outreached herself and ordered her own tombstone when by her wicked wizardry she had the tidings of her man's death at the instant it occurred.

And here again we're forced to make a choice between the natural and the supernatural. That Kundre should have confessed she was guilty was not particularly important.

We know that under heavy mental stress people will accuse themselves of almost any crime. There's hardly a sensational murder case in which the police don't have to deal with numerous entirely innocent self-accusers. That part of it is understandable.

What is more difficult to explain is that at the very moment Peter Grimes broke Kundre's neck the swelling in Abigail Newton's tongue began to subside, and by noon she had entirely regained the power of speech. Indeed, she regained it so fully that within six months she was twice sentenced to the ducking-stool for public scoldings, and finally was forced to stand before the meeting house on the Sabbath with a muzzle on her face and a paper reading 'Common Scold' hung by a string around her neck.

Not the least mystifying thing about the mystery of Kundre Maltby was the way her fortune disappeared. That she and Pelatiah had been rich was common knowledge, but when the assessors went to her house to take her property in custody they could find nothing of substantial value. Not a single gold or silver coin, nor yet a bit of jewellery could they turn up, though they searched the place from cellar to ridgepole and even knocked down several walls in quest of concealed hiding places. So, balked in the attempt to work a forfeiture of her fortune, they sold the house and land at public vendue, put the proceeds in the town treasury and

Is the Devil a Gentleman?

farmed the children out to be taught useful trades.

Micah was apprenticed at the rope-walk owned by Goodman Richard Belkton, Kundre took her place among the sewing maids of Goodwife Deborah Stiles, and except when they were in school or went, well chaperoned, to divine service at the meeting house, they never saw each other.

Their lot was not a happy one. We all know the sadistic cruelty of the young. The lad who goes to a new school today has a hard time until he's proved himself to be the equal of the class bully, or till the novelty of hazing him wears off. But Kundre and her brother had to face the taunts and insults of their classmates endlessly. No one wished to sit with them or share a hornbook with them. If, maddened by the spiteful things said of his mother, Micah fought his tormentor and came off winner, his victory was vociferously attributed to witchcraft. If he lost the fight the victor called on all to witness how Heaven had helped the right in overcoming evil.

Both were apt pupils, but their readiness in reading, ciphering and writing caused no commendation from the schoolma'am. She too believed their aptitude infernally inspired and made no secret of it. So successful recitations were rewarded by an acid reference to their mother's compact with the Evil One. Failure brought a caning.

In all the dreary monotone of life the one highlight for

Kundre was Hosea Newton. It may seem strange that the son of her mother's fiercest persecutor should prove her only friend, but it was no stranger than the contrast between Hosea and his mother. Where she was angular and acid and sharp-tongued he was inclined to plumpness, slow of speech and even-tempered. When all the little girls drew their skirts back from Kundre as from diabolic pollution, he chose a seat beside her on the form, and shared his primer with her and, to the scandal of the class, often gave her tidbits from the ample luncheon which his mother packed for him each morning. When Charity Wilkins accused Kundre of stealing a new thimble from her he found the missing bauble concealed in Charity's pocket and pulled her hair until she admitted her fault. Charity's big brother Benjamin took up the lists for his sister, whereupon Hosea entered combat with enthusiasm and left Benjamin with a bloody nose and greatly chastened tongue.

But this little interlude of friendship had disastrous results. Goodwife Wilkins went to Abigail, who, horrified that her son had espoused the witch-child's cause, took him forthwith to Reverend Silas Middleton, who quoted Scriptual texts to him—'Evil communications corrupt good manners'—exhorted him, prayed over him and finally caned him soundly.

After that Hosea had to content himself with smiling

at Kundre over his primer. All speech between them was forbidden, and though the Reverend Middleton's precepts had made but small impression on Hosea, he had a vivid memory of the thrashing that accompanied them.

The quiet of the lazy years flowed over Danby like a placid river. In the harbour the tall ships shook out their wings and sped to the far corners of the earth and presently came back again with holds filled with strange merchandise. Or perhaps they did not come back, and the women put on mourning clothes and there were new stones in the churchyard, with empty graves beneath them. King Philip's War was fought and won and the settlers needed to fear Indian raids no longer. But in the main life just went on and on. Its groove was deepened, but the course and pattern never changed.

Hosea Newton went away to Harvard College where he was to be trained for the ministry, Micah worked at the rope-walk, harbouring black resentment in his heart, but not daring to give tongue to it; Kundre toiled in Goody Stiles's workroom from sunrise to sunset. She proved a clever needle-woman and her work was eagerly bought up, but had no credit for it. Goodwife Stiles displayed the dresses proudly, and accepted compliments with modest grace, but she never told whose agile fingers fashioned them. In this she showed sound business sense, for many of her customers would have hesitated to wear garments made by a witch-child. And then—

One evening in late summer Kundre lay in Goodman Stiles's oat field. She had worked all day, her eyes and muscles ached, and she was so tired that she could have cried with it, but now she had a little respite. The earth felt warm and comforting to her cramped muscles, she seemed to draw vitality from it while a little breeze played through the bearded grain, making it rustle softly, like a bride's dress.

A bride's dress! Kundre thought. Other maids went to the meeting house or stood up in their own homes in stiff, rustling taffety while the parson joined them to the men of their choice. Was she forever doomed to tread the earth in loneliness, to find no lover, no friend, even, in the whole world? It seemed a hard fate for a maid as well-favoured as she.

Kundre knew that she had beauty. Unlike her mother, she was little; little and slender with grey eyes and a soft-lipped, rather sad smile. Her hair, despite the severe braids in which she wore it, was positively thrilling in its beauty. Paler than her mother's, it had the sweet amber-gold of melted honey in dark lights and the vivid sheen of burnished silver when the sunshine fell on it. There was a sort of aristocratic fragility hinted at by her arched, slender neck and delicately-cut profile, her hands were so slight that she wore child's mittens in cold weather, and the cast-off shoon of neighbours' half-grown daughters were too large for her, even when she wore the thickest woollen stockings.

But now she had kicked off the rough brogans and stripped the heavy cotton stockings off and drew her naked, gleaming feet up under her as she half sat, half lay upon the warm and friendly earth. She rested her elbow upon a bent knee, outlining her chin with her fingers as she looked toward the blue, distant hills. How would it seem, she wondered, to have someone look at her in friendship, speak a kindly word to her, perhaps—her pulses quickened at the daring thought—tell her she was beautiful?

A footstep sounded at the margin of the field and she crouched like a little partridge when it hears the hunter coming. If she were very still, perhaps whoever came would pass her by unseeing. She had no wish to be seen. Since early childhood she had never known a friendly look or word, except—

The footsteps came still nearer, swishing through the nodding grain, and now she heard a man's voice humming softly:

> *Wish and fulfilment can severed be ne'er,*
> *Nor the thing prayed for come short of the prayer—*

'I crave thy pardon, mistress!' Unaware of Kundre crouching in her covet he had almost trodden on her. A flush suffused his face as he stepped backward hurriedly and almost lost his balance in the process.

'I had no business trespassing on Neighbour Stiles's land—why, Kundre, lass, is't truly thou? How lovely thou art grown!' he broke off in surprised delight and to her utter blank amazement, dropped down to the ground beside her. 'It must be full three years since I have seen thee,' he added.

Kundre looked at him in wonder. At first it had been but a man she saw, and men, almost as much as women, were her natural enemies, for she had led an odd and hunted life, and like an animal knew the world of men and women only through the blows it dealt her. But as she looked into the smiling friendly face she felt the blood flow into her cheeks and bring sudden warmth to her brow, for it was Hosea Newton sitting by her in the oat field, Hosea Newton's voice, all rich with friendly laughter, asked how she did, and—her heart beat so that she could hardly breathe—Hosea Newton has just said that she was lovely.

The years had been kind to him. Strongly made, wide-shouldered, he was still not burly, only big; and his face was undeniably handsome. He had a short upper lip and a square jaw with a dimple in it, blue eyes set wide apart beneath dark, curving brows, and lightly curling dark hair that fitted his well-formed head like a cap.

'Art glad to see me?' he asked frankly, and Kundre sat in

thoughtful silence for a while before she answered softly:

'I am not sure, Hosea. In all the world thou art the only person who has spoken kindly to me since my mother—died—but once, I recollect, thou suffered for thy kindness to me. Now—'

'Now,' he mimicked laughing, 'I'll dare the parson or the elders to admonish me. I am my own man, Kundre, and think what thoughts I choose, say what I will and go with whom I please. Aye,' he added as she answered nothing. 'I've thought a deal about things, Kundre, and what I think might not make pleasant hearing for the parson and the elders, or my mother, either. I've seen the Quakers whipped and hanged and branded for their faith's sake, seen helpless, innocent old women go tottering to the gallows tree for witchcraft that they never worked, and could not work, and seen the men who call themselves God's ministers work lustily in Satan's vineyard.'

'Thou thinkest, then—' she asked him with a quaver in her voice—'it may be possible my mother was no witch—'

'No more a witch than any other,' he replied. 'Though I speak of the flesh that bore, me, I say that those who swore her life away are tainted with the blood of innocence—why, Kundre, lass, what aileth thee?'

The girl had flung her arms about him and was sobbing out her heart against his shoulder. For almost twenty years she'd led a pariah's life, hounded, scorned and persecuted, and the memory of her mother had been rubbed into her breaking heart like salt in a raw wound. Now here at last was one who had a kind word for her mother, who dared suggest she had not merited a felon's shameful death.

What happened then was like a chemical reaction in its spontaneity. It may have been that pity which is said to be akin to love inspired him to put his arms about her as she sobbed against his shoulder, but in the fraction of a heart-beat there was no questioning the emotion that possessed him. From him to her, and from her to him, there seemed to flow a mystic fluid—a sort of intangible soul-substance—that met and mingled like the waters of two rivers at their confluence and merged them into each other until they were not twain, but one.

It was an odd idyll, this romance of a man whose childhood had been spent in the house with a bawling woman and this woman whose whole life had been warped by hatred and suspicion. To say that they loved at first sight would not be accurate. Each had carried the image of the other in his heart since childhood, in each the thought of the other had been present constantly, not consciously, any more than they were conscious of the hearts that beat beneath their breasts, but always there, the greatest, most important, most vital thing in either of their lives. Now they were aware of it with blinding, dazzling suddenness. The glory of it almost stunned them.

Every evening when her work for Goody Stiles was done Kundre hurried to the oat field, and always he was there to greet her and come hurrying with uplifted hands to take her in his arms.

Judged by modern free-and-easy standards they were inhibited in their love-making. They hardly kissed at all, and when they did it was a chaste embrace which brother and sister might have exchanged. But she would put her hand in his and turn it till her soft palm rested on his and her little fingers made a soft and gentle pattern of his own, then rest her head against his shoulder till her gleaming hair was on his cheek, its perfume fresh and sweet as that of the green growing things about them.

I said theirs was an odd love. So it was. A love compounded partly of loneliness, partly of heart-hunger, partly of true, honest friendship; not without its moments of passion, but entirely without the savage, selfish hunger of passion; not lacking ecstasy, but with the ecstasy of love fulfilled, not satiated.

They did not talk much. There was small need of words, for that mysterious warm current, strong as a rising ocean tide, flowed constantly between them, fusing their two selves in one. And when they came to say good night the sweet pain of their parting was itself a compensation for the day-long separation facing them.

Then came catastrophe, as dreadful and as unexpected as a thunder-bolt hurled from a cloudless sky. Her brother Micah ran away from his master. It was either flight or murder, for despite the expert way in which he did his work old Goodman Belkton found fault with him constantly, and his fellow 'prentices, not slow to take their cue from the master, taunted him with his mother's conviction and intimated that he used her devilish arts to make his handiwork the best the 'walk turned out.

Runaway apprentices were fair game for anyone, and Goodman Belkton offered a reward of two pounds for the stray's return, so when four sturdy louts saw Micah on the dock at Salem Town, about to sign before the mast for a voyage in the Indies, they set on him and bound him with a length of rope and dragged him back to Danby.

But while they were still in the Danby suburbs they had been set upon by a ferocious heifer that gored one of them sorely, knocked down another, and put them all so utterly to flight that their prisoner escaped and joined his ship at Salem before she sailed with the tide. They brought their wounded comrade into Danby, where, over sundry mugs of potent rum-and-water, they had a wondrous story to relate.

The cow that set on them had been no ordinary cow, it

seemed, but a demon beast whose nostrils breathed forth fiery flames, and which announced *in human words*, 'I'll soon set thee free from this scum, my brother!'

This all happened in the early evening, but before it was too dark for them to see the demon beast go tearing off across a meadow when its fell work had been done and suddenly sit down upon the sod like a woman, straddle a long fence-rail like a witch that mounts a broom, and fly shrieking off across the sky toward Goodman Stiles's oat field.

And where had Kundre been while this was happening? Her mistress asked her pointblank, and pointblank she refused to answer. And there the matter might have rested, perhaps, if Jonathan Sawyer, a labourer of Goodman Williams' plantation, had not volunteered the information that at nine o'clock the night before he's seen her hurrying from Stiles's oat field and heard her singing something not to be found in the hymn book.

It seemed hardly necessary for the constable to call a *posse comitans* of trained bandsmen to arrest her or to summon Parson Middleton to lend them spiritual assistance. But so he did, and with martial clank of sword and pike and musket, and with the Parson with his Book beneath his arm, they went to Goodwife Stiles's house and formally took Kundre into custody, bound her wrists together with the constable's spare bridle, put a horse's leading-strap about her neck and marched her through the streets to Danby jail, where they lodged her with a double guard before the door.

Hosea Newton roused from a deep, dream-tormented sleep, completely conscious, every faculty alert. His room was buried in a darkness blinding as a black cloak, for the moon had set long since, and a cloud-veil obscured the stars. Some instinct, some sentinel of the spirit that stands watch while we are sleeping, told him he was not alone, but he could see or hear nothing.

All day he'd raged through Danby Town like a madman, calling on the parson and the constable and even the high magistrate to intercede for Kundre. She was no witch, he vowed, but a sweet, pure maid who held his heart in the cupped palms of her two little hands. The ruffians who had told the story of the demon heifer were a lot of drunken, craven liars, seeking to excuse their prisoner's escape with this wild tale. He'd prove it; he would range the countryside until he'd found the cow that bested them and lead her singlehanded to the pound for all to see she was a natural beast.

The parson and the constable and magistrate were sympathetic listeners, but one and all refused to help in his trouble. The woman was a witch, the vowed and dedicated votary of Satan—like mother, like daughter. Could any natural cow put four strong men to flight, and they all armed with stout cudgels? And, most especially, could a natural beast bestride a fence-rail and sail through the sky on it? 'Poor boy, thou art bewitched by this vile whelp from Satan's kennels,' they told him.

'But fear not, poor, befuddled lad, tomorrow we shall prove that thy infatuation is the devil's work, for on the town common at sunrise we shall prick the witchling with long pins until we find the devil's mark, and thou shalt see she is in very truth a servant of the Prince of Darkness.'

He'd tried to see her in the jail, but the trained bandsmen turned him back. No one must see the witch until she had passed through the ordeal, even the turnkey was forbidden to go near her or to look into her cell. How should she eat and wherewith should she quench her thirst? Let Beelzebub her master see to that. They were Christian men and had no traffic with the servants of Satan.

Finally, worn out in body and in spirit, he had come home, refused his supper—could he take food while Kundre starved?—and thrown himself upon his bed, full-dressed, to fall into a sleep of utter exhaustion.

Desperate men make desperate plans, and Hosea was desperate. It did not matter to him whether she were good of bad or innocent or guilty. He loved her and would not desert her. If the court found her guilty—and accusation was equivalent to conviction—he would denounce himself as a wizard, and hang with her upon the gallows tree. She should not go to that dark land beyond the grave alone.

What was it? Something stirred in the soft darkness of the room; a shadow moving in the shadows, a rat that came to forage in the dark?

He knew that it was none of these, for in the gloom that blotted out the outlines of the furniture he saw a gleam of light, or rather lightness, like a cloud of faintly luminous vapour swirling from an unseen boiling kettle.

Slowly it spread, wafting upward, and now he saw the outlines of a figure in it, and the blood churned in his ears, his throat grew tight, and at the pit of his stomach he seemed to feel a burning and a freezing, all at once.

'Who—what art thou?' he croaked hoarsely, and the sound of his own frightened voice was terrifying in the haunted darkness.

No answer came to his challenge, but the figure looming faintly in the mist-cloud seemed taking on a kind of substance. Now he could see it quite clearly, and the terror which engulfed him seemed to be an icy flood that paralyzed his heart and brain and muscles.

Yet notwithstanding his terror he felt a kind of admiration for the phantom. It was a woman, tall as a tall man, yet with a calm and regal beauty wholly feminine. Across the low white brow a spate of gold-hued hair fell flowing to her knees, and from the perfect contour of her face great eyes of zenith-blue looked at him under brows of startling blackness. She was dressed in widow's weeds; a chain and pendant of some dull, lack-lustre metal hung about her throat.

He knew her! He has been a little lad scarce eight years old when Goodman Stiles had raised him to his shoulder that he might see the hangman Peter Grimes work the courts sentence on Kundre Maltby, the witch-woman. With a sudden pang of recollection he recalled how he had thought it a great pity that so much beauty should be vowed to Satan and hanged upon the gallows tree and entombed in the earth.

'What—' by supreme effort he forced speech between palsied lips—'what wouldst thou with me, Kundre Maltby?'

'Wilt take my help, Hosea Newton?' asked the spectre, and her voice was cold and desolate as December storm-wind blowing over pine-capped hills.

Hosea hesitated in his answer, and well he might. The wraith, if wraith it were, was that of a condemned witch-woman, hanged for sorcery, and, presumably, made fast in hell. He might have been in advance of his time, but he was part and parcel of his generation, and since Deuteronomy was penned men had regarded witches as disciples of the Evil One. To traffic with them was forbidden under pain of death and loss of soul. This was a witch's ghost, as dreadful as the witch herself, perhaps more dreadful, since she had burned in hell for twenty years, and he must make the choice of taking aid from her or bidding her begone. There was no middle course; he must hold true to all the teachings that had been instilled in him since infancy and bid her avaunt, or make compromise with Evil incarnate and put his soul in dreadful jeopardy—to what end? Did not the writings of the Fathers teach that Satan is the arch-deceiver? Would he keep the compact offered by this messenger from hell?

Then came the thought of Kundre, little Kundre, starved and thirsting, languishing in prison till the morrow, when they'd strip her to her shift in sight of all the town and pierce her tender flesh with long, cruel pins—a thousand thousand years of burning hell would be a bargain-price to pay for her deliverance.

'Say on, O spirit of my Kundre's mother,' he commanded. 'I'll take the help thou offerest me, and pay the price thou asketh.'

The phantom raised one white, almost transparent hand and loosed the medal from its neck. 'Take this,' it bade, and it seemed that its ghostly voice was stronger, warmer. 'Hie with it to the jail house and cut away the bars that pen her in. Then fly across the border southward—my time is sped, I must e'en go!'

The voice stopped suddenly, as though a hand had been

laid on the spectre's throat, and like an April snowflake melting in the rising sun of spring, the faintly-shining vision merged back in the darkness.

He could not say if it had been a vivid dream or if a visitant had come to him, but presently he rose and struck a flint-spark in his tinderbox and lit a tallow dip. There on the floor beside his bed lay a medallion of dull metal, not lead nor iron, but apparently a mixture of the two, fixed to a length of slender chain of the same sheenless substance. Curiously, he noted that his hands were soiled with fresh earth and his fingernails broken, as though he had been burrowing like a woodchuck. Yet he knew he had not left his chamber since he flung himself upon the bed and fell asleep.

Or had he? We may wonder. Might he not have been the victim of somnambulism, and risen to go scraping at the earth that covered Kundre Maltby's body in the churchyard, then, still asleep, come back with the mysterious medal? The thought did not occur to him, but in the light of modern psychological experiments we may entertain it.

At any rate he recognized the medallion and took it in his hand. It was quite plain on one side and engraved with characters he could not read upon the other. Its edge was rounded like that of a milled coin, and though it was no larger than a penny it weighed as much as a gold sovereign.

What was it that the ghost had ordered him to do? Hie

with it to the jail house and cut away the bars that pen her in.'

With this dull piece of soft metal? He was about to fling the medal from him in disgust when the echo of the ghostly voice seemed coming to him through the candlelight-stained darkness. 'Hurry, hurry, lover of the falsely-accused, or it will be too late!'

He knew what cell they'd lodged her in, the same in which her mother languished twenty years ago. It was on the ground floor of the prison, and by standing on his tiptoes he could look through the barred window.

If they caught him skulking round the jail house—What matter? He was resolved to die with her, why not share prison with her ere they hanged him?

Danby jail loomed dimly, a darker darkness in the starless night, as Hosea approached it, treading noiselessly in stockinged feet. 'Kundre,' he whispered softly as he tapped upon the stone sill of her cell window. 'Can'st hear me, dearest love?'

'Is't thou, my very dearest?' the girl's reply came to him through the formless darkness. 'Oh, Hosea—' He heard her sobs, the small, sad sounds of utter misery, as her voice broke.

'Aye, heart o' mine, 'tis I, and I have come to tell thee that thou shalt not go alone—come closer, love, stretch out

43

thy hands to me—'

'I cannot, dearest one; they've chained me to the wall as if I were a rabid cur—'

Hosea clenched his teeth in fury and, unthinking, drove his hand against the prison bars. It was the hand in which he clasped the witch's medal, and as it struck the bar he drew back with a startled exclamation. The heavy, hand-forged iron had melted from contact with the medal as if it had been tallow touched by flame.

In a moment he was sawing at the window-bars with the mysterious coin, cutting them away as if they had been cheese. Silently he laid them on the turf outside the prison window, then, when he had an opening large enough to crawl through, let himself inside the cell and felt his way toward her.

They wasted no time in reunion or premature rejoicings. With her hand on his to guide it he pressed the witch's coin against the iron collar locked around her neck, and laid the fetter on the straw-strewn cell floor carefully, lest its clanking rouse the guard who waited in the corridor outside. Then, step by cautious step, he led her to the window.

Hand in hand they crept along the shadowed street until they reached the stable where his mother's horses stamped before their mangers. In a moment he had saddled the best beast and led it out, swung her to the saddle-bow before him and set out toward the southern boundary of the town. They dared not trot or gallop lest the pounding of the horse's hoofs arouse the neighbours, but presently they reached the churchyard, and he drove his heels into the stallion's flanks.

'Wait, wait, my dear,' she begged him as they passed the white-spired meeting house, 'I would say farewell to my mother ere we shake the dust of Danby from our shoon forever.'

'Aye,' he conceded, lowering her to the ground. 'That is but fitting, sweetling. We are indebted to thy mother for thy liberty tonight.'

Together they walked to the grave, and while the girl knelt on the moss that rimmed the stone he looked down at her pensively. He wondered why his conscience did not trouble him. Tonight he had accepted diabolic aid, made compromise with Evil. Even now he had the witch-wife's medal in his pocket—he drew the flat metallic disc to look at it. Should he take it with him, or return it to the grave? he wondered, then wondered more at what was happening. The coin seem straining at his fingers, as if a thin, invisible thread were pulling it, or it had volition of its own and sought release from his grasp.

But, strangely, the pull was all in one direction, toward the foot of Kundre Maltby's grave.

Wonderingly, he stepped in the direction of the tug, and

noticed that it increased sharply, then seemed to bear straight down toward the earth.

He dropped upon his knees. The coin seemed guiding his hand toward the tombstone and, still marvelling, he reached in the direction that it indicated. His fingers touched the long grass growing by the stone and found an opening like a woodchuck's burrow. Inside was something stiff and hard, yet slightly pliable, like old, oiled leather.

He grasped the object, tugged at it and brought it out. It was a leather sack, well smeared with tallow, stiff with age and long entombment in the earth, but wholly intact. A wax seal held the cord that bound its mouth, but this crumbled as he touched it. Inside were several smaller sacks, some of soft buckskin, some of coarse linen, and in them were bright English sovereigns, round silver Spanish dollars, and gleaming articles of jewellery. The mystery of Kundre Maltby's lost fortune was solved. She had buried it beneath the stone that marked her husband's empty grave, and when they went to scoop the hollow to receive her body they had used only the upper portion of the grave.

Hosea chuckled as he realized what has happened. The diggers' spades had been within a hand's-width of the treasure, yet none had suspected it.

Witchcraft? Perhaps, but very fortunate witchcraft for him and Kundre. A moment since they had had nothing but the clothes they stood in and the stolen stallion; now they were rich. Their life would not be hard—if they could get away.

The night was tiring rapidly as they rode into the woodland. Long streaks of grey were showing in the eastern sky, small noises came to them, the chirp of crickets and the sleepy murmurs of awakening birds, but on and on they rode, secure in the knowledge that Danby jail had no bloodhounds to pursue them, and their escape could not be known till sunrise, for no one, jailer or turnkey or guard, would dare go near the witch's cell till full daylight.

The Newport Quakers greeted them hospitably, and when they found that they had money offered them letters to the first citizens of Philadelphia.

In two days they took passage on a sloop bound for the Delaware, and, once on the high sea, were married by the master. So Kundre Maltby and Hosea Newton, children of seafaring Danby skippers, plighted troth upon the ocean, with the singing of the wind in the rigging for wedding march and the skirling mewl of sea gulls for a prothalamium.

They were not the first, nor, unhappily, the last to be driven from their homes by ignorance and bigotry masquerading as religion, but in Philadelphia they found such peace and happiness as never could have been theirs in New England. Their house stood on a tall hill overlooking the wide Schuylkill and the prosperous little Quaker city, and there their family multiplied until they had four sons and three daughters.

It was an evening in mid-April, the anniversary of her father's death at Captain Newton's hand, if she had known it, that Kundre stood with Hosea on the porch of their mansion and watched the lights of Philadelphia quench out against the darkness. Honora, their last-born daughter, had been christened in the afternoon, and now, all vestige of original sin washed from her, was slumbering as peacefully as any cherub in the nursery.

'Look, heart of mine,' bade Kundre, 'all those good folk go to their rest down yonder. They are a kind and gentle people, and I know their dreams are of a better world.'

'Aye, dearest,' he slipped an arm round her, 'a better world, in truth. Not in some dim, misty Promised Land on t'other side of Jordan, but here in this same world we live in. There'll come a time, my sweet, when men with lofty dreams shall waken at a great tomorrow's dawn and find their dreams still there, and nothing vanished but the night.'

The Bishop brought his story to a close and looked from Dr Bentley to the younger clergyman with a quizzical twinkle in his eye. 'I shan't ask you to pass judgement,' he said. 'Whether Hosea Newton should have scorned the witch's offer—or whether he received it, for that matter—are purely academic questions today. I'm pretty sure though,' he chuckled, 'that if he had refused it I should not be here this evening.'

'How's that, sir?' asked young Dr Kitteringson.

'Well, you see, Hosea Newton was my great-grandfather, several times removed, and his wife, the witch's child, my ancestress. So was the witch, for that matter.'

'And the witch's coin?' asked Dr Kitteringson. 'Do you know what became of it?'

'Yes,' answered Bishop Chauncey. 'Here it is.' He thrust two fingers in his waistcoat and produced a little metal disc which might have been silver, but it wasn't, flat and plain on one side, marked with faint traces of old Nordic runes upon the other. 'I've carried it as a lucky piece for years,' he added. 'My grandfather carried it all through the Civil War and never had a wound; my father had it with him at San Juan Hill and came off without a scratch. I lugged it through the Argonne and came out safely, but once when I left it on my dressing table in Paris I was run down by a taxi-cab before I had a chance to cross the street.'

Dr. Kitteringson was handling the strange coin gingerly, half curiously, half fearfully. 'You've tested it for magic powers?' he asked.

'Good gracious, no son. I don't suppose it has any, and— good heavens, look!'

Young Dr. Kitteringson had taken up the fire shovel and

drawn the coin's blunt edge across its gleaming brass bowl. Where the medal touched the brass it cut a kerf as easily as if it had been pressed through softened tallow.

'Great Scott, Bishop—Dick!' exclaimed Dr Bentley. 'What do you think of that?'

The Bishop dropped the witch's coin back in his waistcoat pocket and held his glass out toward his host. His hand was shaking slightly, but his eyes and voice were steady. 'I think I'd like another drop of brandy; quickly, if you please,' he answered.

AUTHOR'S NOTE

Is the Devil a Gentleman? is a question story. Whether Kundre Maltby was a witch at all, whether she appeared as a ghost to her future son-in-law, whether he actually compromised with evil or whether he was the victim of a vivid dream and a case of somnambulism—all these are questions which are continually raised through the course of the story.

Like an advocate, I've merely presented the evidence in the case, but unlike an advocate, I've forborn to argue from the evidence; hence the fury of readers must reach their verdict without help or hints from me.

Background for the story: Turn to page 117 of the Cambridge edition of the poems of John Greenleaf Whittier. There it all is, beautifully outlined for you, except for the Bishop, and the

witch's coin and a few little things which I thought up myself.
SEABURY QUINN

FRANCE—THE HOME OF BLACK MAGIC

'*From the thirteenth century downwards, Southern France was regarded as the nursery of heresy and the Black Art, to which its location on the Mediterranean and in the vicinity of Spain particularly contributed—Spain being regarded as the proscribed land of magic and Saracenic heresy. Thus the oldest relation of the Witch Sabbath lays the scene of it in Southern France; and Alphonso de Spina records that proselyted women in Dauphiné were seduced by the devil by night into a wilderness where they worshipped a he-goat upon a rock by torchlight. The notorious Witch Sabbath of Arras in 1495, at about which time de Spina lived, was frequented by men, while in the more ancient times it was only resorted to by women. This celebration continued in France, especially in the Southern provinces, for many centuries. In the reign of Charles IX, the great sorcerer so much dreaded, Rinaldo des Trois Echelles, was executed, and he said undauntedly before the King that in France he had three hundred thousand confederates, all of whom they could not commit to the flames as they did him.*'

C. L. ENNESMOSER,
The History of Magic

MONSIEUR SEEKS A WIFE

MARGARET IRWIN

Note.—The following story is an extract from the private memoirs of Monsieur de St. Aignan, a French nobleman living in the first half of the eighteenth century.

I was twenty-four years of age when I returned in 1723 at the end of my three years' sojourn at the English Court, and had still to consider the question of my marriage. My father sent for me soon after my return and asked if I had yet given any thought to the matter. I replied that as a dutiful son I had felt it would be unnecessary and impertinent to do so. My father was sitting in his gown without his wig, for the day was not, and as he sipped his chocolate he kept muttering, 'Too good—too good by half.'

I flicked my boots with my whip and did my best to conceal my impatience, for there was a hunt in the woods at Meudon and I feared I might miss it.

Presently he said, 'There was no one in England with whom you might have wished to form an alliance?'

'No, sir. The English actresses are charming.'

This time he seemed better pleased for he repeated, 'Good, good. That is an admirable safeguard to your filial duty in marriage.'

He then threw me over a letter from an old friend of his, the Comte de Riennes, a man of little fortune but of one of the oldest families in the kingdom. I skimmed two pages of compliments and salutations which seemed tedious to me after the shorter style of English correspondence, and got to the body of the letter. It was in answer to a proposal from my father that the two houses should be united by my marriage with one of the three daughters of the Comte.

He expressed warmly his gratitude and pleasure and told my father that as he had only enough fortune to bestow a *dot* on one of his daughters, the two others would enter a convent as soon as their sister was married; the choice of the bride he very magnanimously left to my father, and my father with equal magnanimity now left it to me. As I had seen and heard of none of them, I was perfectly indifferent.

'My motives are entirely disinterested' I said to my father. 'I only wish to make a match that will be in accordance with your wishes and those of such an old friend of the family as Monsieur le Comte de Riennes. We had better therefore refer the choice back to him.'

As I said this, I turned the last page of the letter, and saw that Monsieur le Comte suggested that I should pay a visit to* the Château de Riennes in the country of the Juras and see the three daughters for myself before deciding which I should marry. The generosity of this offer struck me forcibly and I at once accepted it. My father also remarked on the openness and liberality of his old friend, and observed that as in the usual course the eldest would have been appointed to the marriage, it would show justice and delicacy in me to choose her, unless of course she had a hump back or some other deformity; 'though in that case,' he remarked, 'she would surely have been placed in a convent long before.'

I went out to find that I was too late for the hunt at Meudon. It was the Regent* who informed me of this, for I met him strolling up and down one of the corridors in the palace and gaping out of the windows for all the world like an idle lackey. He was then very near the end of his life, though he was not old, and I remember being struck by his bloated aspect and thinking to myself, 'If that man should have a fit, I would not bet a button on his life.'

He did me the honour to ask me many questions about England, especially the rapid advance of scientific discovery in which he took a great interest.

'How times have changed!' he remarked. When I was young, I was regarded as a monster and a poisoner because I was an atheist and dabbled in chemistry. Also in black magic; it was the fashion then,' he added. "One must have some superstition, though I dare say you find it inconsistent to discard the superstition of religion, yet to retain that of sorcery.'

As he likes nothing so much as plain speaking, I owned to this, and added in explanation that in England the superstition of magic had for some time been confined to the ignorant and vulgar.

He then remarked on my approaching marriage (for my father had spoken of it to him) and, turning back just as he was leaving me, he said, The French Juras were a dangerous country once. Take care of yourself there.'

His voice always sounded as though he were joking, but his melancholy and bloodshot eyes looked serious. I knew that a savage country like the Juras was likely to be infested with robbers, but I should ride well attended and said so. The Regent only smiled, and it suddenly struck me as he walked away that the danger he was thinking of was not connected with robbers, and I could not guess what it was. I did not see him again before his sudden death, and three days later I set out on my journey.

The roads were bad and the inns worse, and I thought with regret of England, which seemed, especially at the worst inn, to be my adopted country. After an endless and dreary plain cultivated by wretched peasantry, I saw the rugged shapes of the Jura mountains against the sky and knew I was reaching my journey's end. The next day our horses were toiling steadily uphill, and the road was rougher, the countryside more deserted than ever. We entered a forest of dark pine trees which shed a gloomy twilight over our path, for it could now only by courtesy be termed a road. I began to be certain that we had missed our way, when I saw a creature approaching us who seemed to be human more from his upright position on two legs than from anything else in his appearance. I asked if we were on the road for Riennes, and though we had the greatest difficulty in understanding his dialect, it was at last clear that we were. He seemed, however, to be warning us not to take the wrong path farther on, and walked back a little way in order, I supposed, to direct us.

I dropped him some money for his trouble and he then repeated his warnings with what struck me as extraordinary urgency and even anxiety. He talked faster and more unintelligibly until the only word I could be certain of was the continual repetition of the name 'Riennes,' and he wagged his shaggy beard and rolled his eyes as he said it, with an expression that seemed positively that of fear or horror. I concluded that he was probably half-witted, and threw him another coin to get rid of him. At this he laid hold on my bridle and said two or three times, very slowly and as distinctly as he could. 'Do not go to Riennes.'

Convinced by now that the fellow was mad, I struck his hand off my bridle and rode on.

We came out of the forest to find ourselves surrounded by dark hills that rose sharply from the ground in jagged and hideous shapes. Their slopes were bare and uncultivated and many of their summits were crowned with frowning rocks. As I rode through this desolate and miserable country, a deep depression settled on me. I had for some time been feeling the regrets that most young men experience when the time comes for them to arrange their affairs and decide on marriage.

I was not yet sufficiently advanced in age or experience to consider youth and innocence the most attractive qualities in woman. But these would probably be the only charms in the raw country girl I was to marry, besides good health and perhaps rustic beauty.

I had heard much of the unutterable tedium of the lives of the smaller nobility on their country estates, a tedium only to be surpassed by the monotony of the religious life, which poverty enforces so large a proportion of our daughters and younger sons to enter.

Incongruously enough, I wondered at the same moment whether the eldest sister had red hands, and could have wept when it occurred to me that they might be no monopoly but general to all.

I thought with longing of my life and friends in London, of supper parties I had given on the stage, graced by the incomparable Mrs. Barry, the admirable Mrs. Bracegirdle, of the company at White's coffee-house where the conversation was often as good as in Mr. Congreve's comedies, of discussions on politics, philosophy, science, between men of wit and reason. But the melancholy that had now fastened on me was deeper than mere regret, and I could neither account for it nor shake it off.

We had to ask the way to Riennes more than once, and it struck me that the people who directed us showed more than the usual astonishment and awe natural to the peasant in an uncivilized country when suddenly confronted by a noble stranger and his retinue. In fact they seemed to show definite fear amounting sometimes even to terror, so that I was inclined to think that the old Comte must be a harsh and cruel lord to his people.

Towards evening we entered a gorge where our path went uphill between precipitous slopes and vast overhanging crags of dark rock. They were huger and more horrid than anything I could have imagined, and in the stormy twilight (for the clouds hung low and completely covered the taller hills) they presented an aspect that would have been terrifying to a weak and apprehensive imagination. We seemed no bigger than flies as our horses crawled up the steep ascent. A beetling crag overhung our path, and as I turned the sharp corner that it made, my mare suddenly reared and backed so violently that I was nearly thrown.

I urged her on with all my force and as I did so I glanced up and saw that what must have frightened her was the figure of a girl standing on the slope of the hill some way above us. She stood so still that at first glance she would have been indistinguishable from the rocks that surrounded her, had it not been for her long pale hair that the wind was blowing straight forward round her face. She wore a wreath of pale lilac and blue flowers, and I could just seize a glimpse of eyes that seemed the same colour as the flowers, set in a white face, before her hair blew past and hid it completely.

That glance was all I could give, for my mare was rearing and plunging in a manner utterly foreign to her usual behaviour. Suddenly, however, she stood quite still, trembling and bathed in sweat. I seized the opportunity to look up again, but the figure had gone. So still had she been while there, and so suddenly had she disappeared, that for an instant I doubted my senses and wondered if my eyes had played me some trick in that dim confusion of lights and shadows. But my impression of her had been too vivid for this doubt to last; I could even recollect the dark dress she wore, plainly cut like a peasant's. Yet I could not think of her as peasant, nor as a person of quality. She seemed some apparition from another world, and though I laughed at myself for my romantic fancy, I defy the most reasonable philosopher not to have shared it if he had seen her as I did. My mare certainly appeared to hold my opinion and with the greater conviction of terror, for she sidled most ridiculously past the place where the girl had stood, and was sweating and shivering as I rode her on. And what struck me as still more peculiar, all my men had some difficulty in getting their horses to pass that spot.

Half an hour later we were free of that hideous gorge, and could seen the towers of the Château de Riennes pointing upwards above the fir trees on the hill before us. Relief at reaching the end of my journey fought with an apprehension I could not understand. I remember an attempt at reassurance by telling myself, "If my wife plagues me, I can leave her on my estates in St. Aignan, and spend my time in London and Paris.' But even this reflection failed to encourage me.

We clattered into the courtyard to be met with acclamations from grooms and the lackeys who hurried forward to take our horses. The Comte himself came out to the steps of the château and stood awaiting me. He embraced me warmly and led me into the lighted hall with many expressions of welcome and friendship. He looked a much older man than I had expected in a comtemporary of my father's, and his mild blue eyes certainly gave me no impression of the sternness I had anticipated from the timid behaviour of the peasantry.

Indeed there was a certain timidity in his own bearing, a weakness and vacillation in all his movements, as though he lived in continual and fearful expectation. But this did not in any way detract from the courtesy and cordiality of his reception of me and I might not have remarked it had I not been prepared for such a different bearing.

He led me to my room to remove the stains of travel and arrange my dress before being presented to the ladies of his family. Though early in the autumn the weather was cold, and a bright fire of pine logs blazed in my chimney. It was a relief to be sitting in a decent room once more, to have my riding-boots pulled off at last, and to put on a peruke that had been freshly curled and scented.

My valet was a useful fellow and soon effected a satisfactory change in my appearance. I put on a suit of maroon-coloured velvet with embroidered satin waistcoat which I flattered myself set off my figure to advantage, and as I arranged my Mechlin ruffles before a very fine mirror, my gloomy apprehensions lifted, and it was with quite a pleasurable excitement that I looked forward to making the choice of my bride. I laughed at myself for my certainty that one or all would have ugly hands, and reflected that I should probably find a very good, pretty sort of girl and one that in this lonely place was not likely to be entirely unsusceptible.

Madame la Comtesse awaited me in a vast salon of a style that would have been old fashioned in the time of our grandfathers. The huge carved chair in which she sat, raised on a dais in semi-royal fashion at the end of the room, only served to make her appear the more insignificant. Her grey head was bowed, her long knotted fingers hung limply over the arms of her chair. But when she rose to greet me it was with the regal dignity that I remember my mother had told me quite old ladies had had in the days of her youth, a dignity that passed out of fashion with the late Queen Regent*, and is never seen now.

I was shocked, however, at the vacant yet troubled expression in her dim grey eyes. She certainly did not look as old as the Comte, nor could she, I knew from what my father had told me, be far past the period of middle life. Yet her mind seemed feeble and wandering as in extreme age.

She made me sit on a stool beside her chair and strove to entertain me with a courtesy that could still charm, though I could perceive very plainly the effort that it cost her. Every now and then she would stoop to caress a great white cat that rubbed against her chair and make some remark to it or to me concerning it.

I did my best to make friends with the favourite, but I do not like cats, and this beast regarded me with a distant and supercilious air, impervious to all my advances though it never took its pale green eyes off my face. This persistent stare irritated me till I longed to kick it out of the room, and foolishly this irritation somehow prevented me accommodating myself as well as I might have done to my hostess's tentative and desultory conversation.

It was a relief as well as an excitement when Mademoiselle de Riennes and Mademoiselle Marie de Riennes were announced. A tall girl entered the room with her arm around a light childish figure whose face was almost hidden against her sister's sleeve. The elder received my salutations with a certain amount of grace and finish, the younger with such confusion of shyness that in kindness I withdrew my eyes from her as soon as possible.

I was too anxious to see the elder to be able to see very clearly at first, but I perceived that she was neither ugly nor foolish and the hand I was permitted to kiss was of a good shape and colour. Later as we talked I saw that there were certain points in her face and figure that might be called beautiful. Her olive complexion lacked colour, but that could be easily remedied. She had large dark eyes of a very fine shape a well-formed bust and shoulders, a pretty mouth with good teeth, an excellent forehead and charming little ears. Yet the whole did not somehow make for beauty. It was incomplete or perhaps marred in some way.

It is difficult to perceive the habitual expression of a

young girl who is anxious to please, but I thought that the quick interest and smiles with which she attended to my conversation with her mother were not natural to her, and that from time to time a look of sullen and even fierce brooding would settle on her face, though momentarily, for the next instant she would rouse herself and seem to push it away.

Whenever I could do so without increasing her confusion, I stole a look at the younger daughter. She undoubtedly, was possessed of beauty, of a fair, almost infantile order; her lips were full and red and remained always just parted, her face was an exquisitely rounded oval, and her light-brown hair curled naturally on the nape of her neck in tendrils as soft and shining as those of a very young child. But she was extremely unformed, and I could not but feel that in spite of my vague disappointment in the elder, it was she who was in most respects the more suitable for my purpose.

After allowing sufficient time for her to compose herself, I addressed some simple remark to Mademoiselle Marie that should have been perfectly easy to answer. She looked at me with an uncertain, almost an uncomprehending expression in her blue eyes that reminded me of her mother's, and stammered a few words unintelligibly. Her extreme timidity was perhaps natural to her youth and upbringing, but I thought I detected a vacancy and weakness of mind in her manner of showing it.

'Decidedly,' I told myself, 'this one is best fitted for the convent, and after answering my remark myself as though I had but intended to continue it, I addressed myself again to the eldest. She replied very suitably and prettily and I thought her manners would not be amiss in any salon in London or Paris.

We continued happily therefore in a conversation which if not exactly amusing was at least satisfactory and promising, when an absurdly small incident occurred that proved oddly disconcerting to Mademoiselle.

The cat, which had so far continued to reserve its obnoxious gaze for me, suddenly walked across to her stool, looking up in her face and mewing. She shrank back with an involuntary shudder. It was not this that startled me, for I knew many people have an unconquerable aversion to cats and I have seen the great and manly Duc de Noailles turn faint at the Council Board because the little King* carried in a kitten. But what surprised me in Mademoiselle de Riennes was the same backward, fearful glance that I had seen in her father, as though she dreaded, not the cat itself, but some unseen horror behind her. The next moment, however, she was replying naturally and with no more than a becoming hesitation to some remark I had addressed to her.

I wondered why the third daughter had not appeared,

and the same wonder seemed to be disturbing my hostesses for they looked continually towards the door. Madame la Comtesse remarked two or three times, 'My daughter is late'; it was odd that she should so speak of her youngest daughter instead of reserving the expression for Mademoiselle de Riennes. She started violently when the footman announced, 'Mademoiselle Claude de Riennes,' and the eldest daughter leaned suddenly forward as though she would speak to me. She did not, but she fixed on me a look of such agonized entreaty that it arrested me as I rose, so that I did not turn on the instant, as I should have done, to greet Mademoiselle Claude.

When I did, I had to wait a full minute or two before I could recover sufficient composure to address her as I ought. Mademoiselle Claude was the girl I had seen on the rocky hillside. Her smooth and shining hair was dressed high in the prevailing fashion, her hooped dress of pearl-coloured satin was suitable to her rank, yet I was certain that she was the same as that wild figure I had seen, with hair blown straight before her face.

What further startled me was that I found that until that moment I had not really believed the apparition on the hillside to be a human creature. It was a disturbing discovery for a man of sense, living in an age of science and reason, to make in himself. I had certainly never before been guilty of imagining that I had seen a spirit.

I could only conclude that the peculiar gliding grace with which she advanced and curtsied to me did indeed connect her with the nymphs of mountain and grove in classic lore, and considered how I should turn a compliment to her on the subject without exposing to her family how I had met her in this strange fashion.

To my astonishment, however, she said in answer to her mother's introduction, 'I have already seen Monsieur de St. Aignan,' but no surprise was shown by mother or sisters. Mademoiselle Claude's voice was low and very soft, it had a quality in it that I have not met in any other voice and that I do not know how to describe; I should perhaps do so best if I said that it seemed to purr.

She sat beside her mother and did not speak again; her eyes were downcast and her long pale lashes, only less pale than her skin, languished on her cheek; her face was small and round, ending in a sharply pointed little chin. She wore in her bosom a bunch of the same light lilac and blue flowers that had been in her hair when I had first seen her, and the peculiarity of wearing such a simple posy when in full dress, caught my attention.

I asked their names, hoping to hear her speak again, but she only smiled, and it was the eldest daughter who told me that they were wild flowers, harebells and autumn crocuses, and that the latter with their long white stems and fainly purple heads were called Naked Ladies by the shepherd folk. Mademoiselle Claude raised her head as her sister spoke and handed me one to see. Her eyes looked full into mine for an instant and again I could not be certain if their pale colour were more like the blue or the lilac flowers, and again the compliment that rose to my lips evaded me before I could speak it.

The cat had deserted the chair of Madame la Comtesse and was rubbing backwards and forwards against Mademoiselle Claude, at last taking its eyes off my face and staring up at its young mistress. It was evident that she had no share of her sisters aversion to cats. Suddenly it leapt up on to her shoulder and rubbed its head against her long slim throat. Madame de Riennes stroked her daughters head and that of the cat. 'They are both so white, so white,' she murmured, and then, speaking I suppose to me, though she did not appear to be addressing anyone, she said, 'The moon shone on my daughter when she was born.'

I was embarrassed how to reply, for these disconnected remarks seemed to indicate premature senility more clearly than anything she had yet said. Fortunately at this moment the Comte entered and we went to supper.

I sat of course between my hostess and Mademoiselle de Riennes whom I wished to engage again in conversation. But her former ease seemed to have departed, she answered me with embarrassment and sometime? with positive stupidity. She now avoided meeting my eyes and looked repeatedly across the table to where her sisters sat opposite. I could not be sure which of the two she was looking at, for both sat silent with their eyes downcast.

The rest of the evening was spent in the salon, where Madame la Comtesse requested her daughters to show me some of the results of the labours that filled their days. Mademoiselle de Riennes led me to a tapestry frame that struck me as the most perfect exhibition of tedium that could be devised. Mademoiselle Marie showed me a Book of Hours that she was illuminating; my admiration was reserved for the fair fingers that pointed out their work. If the hands of Mademoiselle de Riennes were good, the hands of Mademoiselle Marie were delicious, not so fine in shape, but softly rounded, helpless and dimpled like a baby's. I began to wonder if I might not have judged nastily of her parts. Though the second in age, she appeared the youngest of the three; she was evidently slow in development, and who could tell but that after marriage had placed her in a suitable position, she might become the most brilliant as well as the most beautiful of all?

Politeness obliged me to turn at last to Mademoiselle Claude who was sitting as still as ever, with hands folded in her lap, and ask what she had to show me.

'Nothing, Monsieur,' said she, smiling, but without looking up.

'Mademoiselle is so idle?' I asked, hoping to tease her into a glance. But I did not win it, and at that moment Madame de Riennes suggested we should dance. It proved impossible as the daughters did not know the modern fashion of dancing and I knew no other. Madame de Riennes sat at the harpsichord and played an old-fashioned air to which her two elder daughters danced a *pas de deux*. I was surprised to see that again Mademoiselle Claude did not perform, and asked her if she did not like dancing.

'Oh, yes, Monsieur,' she replied, in that soft purring voice of hers, 'I like it very well.'

'Then do you not care to dance with two or three?'

'Monsieur is right, I prefer to dance with many.'

'Then, Mademoiselle, you can have but few opportunities for dancing here where I should imagine balls are a rarity. Do you not find it very dull?'

'No, Monsieur, I do not find it dull.'

All the time she seemed to be smiling, though as I was standing above her and her face remained lowered, I could not well see. The hands that lay so still in her lap were like the long white stems of the flowers she wore with the ridiculous name—they were so slim and bloodless. As I looked at them

I felt an unaccountable wish to draw away from them. I could in no way explain it; I have felt repulsion to hands before now, but to none that were beautiful. But I decided quickly that it was only an absurd fancy that likened them in my mind to hands of the dead, and so still and white they were that this was not surprising.

When the dance was finished, Madame de Riennes rose from the harpsichord and patted Mademoiselle Claude's cheek.

'My daughter can sing and play,' she said. 'She sits so still, too still, but she can sing very well.'

Mademoiselle Claude fetched her lute. As she sat with the instrument on her knee, her limp fingers plucking idly at the strings, I thought to myself, 'She is the last I would choose to be the mother of my heirs.' There seemed nothing alive about her, from her dead hair, so nearly white, to her pale and smiling lips. In the corner of the wainscot where she sat, her pearl-coloured skirts spread round her and reflected on the polished floor, she had the appearance of a moonlit cloud, possessing no doubt a certain strange beauty but more as a picture than a woman.

She began to sing; I did not think a great deal of her voice, having heard better, but it had a certain charm, being low, caressing and of a peculiar timbre. She sang an air from an opera now out of date, and then a song in which the tune was unlike any other I had ever heard. It was very simple and had a certain gaiety, it seemed to follow no known rules of method and harmony. There were two or three notes that recurred again and again like a call, and the melody between moved backwards and forwards as in the movement of a dance.

It seemed older than any other music, I cannot say why, unless it was that as I listened, my imagination conjured up visions of sacrificial dances performed in the most ancient times of Greece or Egypt. While in England, I had stayed at a country house whose owner had had the humour to take an interest in the old songs and ballads of his countryside and even to profess to admire them. He had played some of them to me one evening when he had tired of the cards, and I could not but admit that there was something in their rude simplicity that pleased the ear.

They were for the most part wild and plaintive, frequently unutterably dismal. But old as they had sounded, this tune that Mademoiselle Claude was singing seemed infinitely older. There was nothing plaintive in its wildness. It belonged to an age when men had riot yet learned to regret, to distinguish between good and evil, to encumber themselves with the million hindrances and restrictions that separate men from beasts.

A strange restlessness and discontent seized on me. I

felt a ridiculous but none the less powerful loathing of my condition, of the condition of all men in this dull world, of the morals and customs that force our lives into a monotonous pattern from the cradle to the grave, of the very clothes I wore, stiff and cumbrous, crowned with a heavy peruke of false hair. I longed to fling them all off and shake myself free, and with them every convention that bound me to decency of conduct. In committing these words to paper, I am aware that I am describing the sensations of a lunatic and a savage rather than any that should be possible to a man of birth, sense and cultivation, living in a highly civilized and enlightened age. But if I am to be truthful in these memoirs I must admit that at the moment I failed completely to observe how shamefully, and, what perhaps is worse, how absurdly inappropriate my sentiments were to a gentleman and a courtier.

I raised my eyes to find those of Mademoiselle Claude fixed upon my face. She was still singing, but I could not distinguish the words nor even recognize to which language they belonged. Her gaze did not startle me for I seemed to know that it had been resting on me for some time. I saw that her eyes, in this light at any rate, were neither blue nor lilac as I had thought, but pale green like those of the white cat that stood, arched and purring, on the arm of her chair; and, like the cat's, the pupils were perpendicular.

Heedless of manners, I looked hard to assure myself of the fact; and her eyes which had been so bashfully abased all the evening did not flicker nor turn away under my stare but continued to gaze into mine until I became conscious of nothing but their pale and luminous depths. They seemed to grow and to diminish, to come near and to recede very far away, and all the time the tune she sang moved up and down as in the measure of a dance, and the words she sang remained unintelligible yet gradually appeared to be familiar.

Suddenly the song ceased, and I started involuntarily and shook myself as though I had been rudely awakened from an oppressive dream. I looked around me, hardly able to believe that my surroundings had remained the same from the time when Mademoiselle Claude had begun to sing. Mademoiselle Marie, seated on a low stool next to her elder sister, was leaning so close against her that her face was completely hidden and her whole body was as stiff and motionless in its crouched position as if it had been paralyzed.

Mademoiselle de Riennes sat as still as she, but her eyes now raised themselves to mine slowly and with difficulty and I caught a glimpse of the same expression of agonized entreaty that had arrested me when I first rose to greet her youngest sister. It was only a glimpse, for the next instant they fell again as though not bearing to look longer into mine. In some way that I must fail to express, she appeared smaller and more insignificant. I wondered that I had ever thought of her as possessing good looks and distinction of manners.

Madame de Riennes had fallen into a doze and it may have been this that gave her, too, a slightly shrunken appearance. Certainly it struck me that she was much older and feebler than I had comprehended. I do not remember how I took my leave of them for the night, I only remember Madame la Comtesse murmuring weakly as she wished me good rest, 'She is so white, my daughter—too white, too white.'

The comfort of a good bed again after so long and uncomfortable a journey was by far my most important reflection on reaching my room, and as my valet prepared me for that blessed condition, the experiences and fancies of the past evening resolved themselves into the opinion that my imagination had been highly strung by the fatigues of the journey and the strangeness of new surroundings, and that in reality the family of the de Riennes were a very good, kindly, though old-fashioned sort of people, and that I had three pretty girls to choose from, though it was still a little difficult to know which to choose.

'Mademoiselle Marie is the prettiest,' I told myself on climbing into bed. 'But Mademoiselle de Riennes has the most sense,' I added, as Jacques drew the curtains round me, 'and Mademoiselle Claude'—I began as I laid my head on the pillows, but I found that I had not known what I thought of Mademoiselle Claude and was just dropping off to sleep without troubling to consider the question when I remembered that I had noticed something very strange about her eyes when she was singing.

For a moment I could not recall what it was, then suddenly it occurred to me, and with a sensation of horror that I had not felt at all at the time I had observed it, that the pupils of. the eyes instead of being round were long and pointed.

I was exceedingly sleepy when I thought of this, but I woke myself by repeating several times as though it were of urgent importance that I should remember it—'The eyes are not human. Remember, the eyes are not human.'

I repeated it until I forgot what it was that had struck my observation, yet it seemed an imperative necessity that I should remember what it was that had filled my whole being with that sense of utmost horror. In my efforts to do so I fell sound asleep.

Nothing is more irritating than to be wakened out of a deep and dreamless slumber by some small, persistent noise. The noise I heard in my sleep kept awakening me again and again until at last, tired of perpetually dropping off and being aroused, I sat up in bed and listened. I heard something rustling outside my door, a soft running tread every now and then up and down the passage, and then, what I knew had awakened me so many times, something scratching at the door itself. I decided I must go and see what it was but felt the most absurd and shameful reluctance to do so.

I put out my hand through the curtains to reach for my bedgown on the chair beside me. Instead of the accustomed touch of velvet and fur that I expected, my hand seemed to be grasping a long cold finger. I recoiled in violent agitation, and as I snatched my hand away and covered it with my other as though to assure myself of a human touch, I thought I felt the finger drawn slowly across my forehead.

I shuddered from it, and yet my horror was mingled with an inexplicable pleasure. Trembling with excitement rather than with fear, I now drew aside the bed curtains, leapt out and opened the shutters.

The moon was nearly at the full, and by its brilliant light I could see, laid on my bedgown, the white and slender stalk of the wild autumn crocus that Mademoiselle Claude had presented to me. It surprised me, for I had no recollection of laying it there and indeed thought I had dropped it into the fire. In any case there was a satisfactory explanation of the cause of my ridiculous terrors, and the touch on my forehead must have been an imaginary result of them. It was odd, though, that as I took up the flower, the sensation of it seemed completely different from the thing that I had first grasped, and I marvelled that I could ever have mistaken it for a human finger.

All was so silent now that I got back into bed, first laying my sword on the chair beside me, and was just falling asleep when again I heard the rustle outside, and a soft stroking rather than scratching, against my door. I stretched out my hand for the sword and found that it was shaking. This evidence of my womanish apprehension was so unaccountable and utterly confounding that I began to wonder if I were not already paying the price, though certainly an over-heavy one, of the pleasures naturally pertaining to a gallant man.

I resolved that now I was about to marry, I would make a different disposition of my life, abandon such pleasures, and settle on my country estates at St. Aignan. At this moment I heard that same furtive noise again on the door, and the idea that my plans for reforming were the result of the scratchings of a cat caused me to burst into a roar of laughter which wholesomely restored me to my natural self.

I snatched up my sword and ran to the door. I could see nothing but darkness, but I heard a faint 'miaow' somewhere down the passage and went quickly and cautiously towards it, calling 'Puss, Puss, Puss,' laughing to myself at the thought of the murder I was contemplating on the favourite of two of my hostesses, and already planning the apology I should have to make. The door into my moonlit room had swung to after me and I had to feel my way in the blackness. Suddenly

I felt claws round my leg and knew that the cat must have rushed at me from behind. I struck quickly down with my sword and thought I hit something soft and springing but could not be quite sure. There was no savage 'miaow' in response to show I had hurt the brute.

I went back to my room and on examining my sword in the moonlight, found that there was a small streak: or blood on it. I thought with satisfaction that that would probably keep the beast away from my door, and settled myself for sleep. I was wrong, for all night I was disturbed by subdued sounds of scampering and scuffling in the passage, and more than once I thought that I felt the lightest pressure of a cold finger on my eyelids.

When Jacques brought me my chocolate in the morning, he found me more worn out and irritable than after a night of debauch. He exclaimed when he saw my sword on which the blood had dried, and I told him to clean it, saying that the cat had been disturbing my rest and that I had struck at it. My head throbbed and ached so uncomfortably that I decided I would refresh myself with a good ride before meeting any of my host's family, and ordered my mare to be saddled at once.

As I went down into the courtyard, I saw the white cat sleeping in a sunny corner of the steps. I turned the animal over with my boot, and it stretched out its paws and clawed playfully at the air. I could discover no sign of any wound anywhere upon it. I asked the groom what other cats they had, and he replied that this was the only one in the château. I got into the saddle, too much mystified to care to think, and rode as hard as I could.

The morning was fresh and pleasant, and the country looked excellent for boar-hunting. I was wondering what entertainment in that way my host meant to show me after my long abstinence (sport in England being of the tamest) when my attention was struck by a huge stone a little way off. I was riding across a fairly smooth slope of moorland with hills on my right that rose in abrupt and monstrous shapes as though thrown up by some violent cataclysm of the earth, while on my left stretched a vast plain as far as I could see. The whole was desolate because uncultivated, but in the morning sunshine the hideous aspect of the country did not oppress one as in the gloomy twilight in which I had first seen it. The stone I had noticed was conspicuous for its size and solitariness, for there were no rocks near.

I was riding up to it when suddenly my mare behaved in exactly the same manner as the evening before, shying violently and then rearing and plunging. I succeeded at last in quieting her sufficiently to keep still, but it was beyond my power to make her advance another step. I had always treated her with the consideration due to a lady of high breeding and mettlesome spirit, but on this occasion I must admit her whims drove me to a pretty considerable use of whip and spur. But all to no effect. She would not advance one step nearer the stone.

I dismounted and was about to see whether I could drag her thither by the bridle, when I noticed footprints at my feet, just in front of my mare's forefeet that were so obstinately planted on the ground. There was nothing odd in finding footprints on the moor, but what was odd was that they did not advance straight in any direction but curved sharply round. I followed them a little way and saw that the marks were exceeding confused, as though many pairs of feet had trodden close upon each other in the same spot. The grass, in fact, was all kicked up, and when I had followed this rough curve a little distance I saw that it was part of the outline of a vast circle in which the stone was, more or less accurately, the centre point.

I had no sooner made this perplexing discovery than I observed a respectable-looking man in black approaching me, whom I presently perceived to be a priest. He greeted me in an abrupt and not over-respectful fashion, asking if I were not afraid to go so near the fairy ring. Few people, he said, would care to adventure themselves so close to it even in broad sunlight. I observed, smiling, that the fairies in this part of the world must be remarkably substantial to have kicked up the ground so vigorously, and asked if he could not give me some more reasonable explanation of the footprints. He looked at me with a suspicious kind of sullen stupidity that made me conclude he was probably very little above the level of a peasant himself.

I left him to walk over to the stone, which I examined with some interest. The ground had been much disturbed close under it, and the stone itself, which was at the top like a table, was covered with dark stains. It occurred to me that here was a possible explanation of my mare's refusal to approach any nearer. Horses are notoriously sensitive to the smell of blood, and I was certain that the stains I was looking at were those of dried blood. I went back to the priest and asked him what the stone was used for.

'It is never used, Monsieur,' he cried, 'no one in the country would go near it.'

'Then,' said I, 'what are those dark stains on it?'

His little dark eyes looked at me anxiously and shiftily as though he disliked the subject.

'A holy man and a son of the Church, Monsieur, can know nothing of such things. Some say that this stone is haunted by devils and that they or the fairies, who resemble them dance in a ring round it.' He crossed himself and continued, 'I say that it is better not to speak of these things but to pray against temptation and the wiles of the Devil and to implore the help and protection of Holy Church.' He added that he was the *curé* of Riennes and chaplain to the convent near by, and invited me to look at his church which was not far off. I found myself walking with him, more out of inattention than politeness, my horse's bridle on my arm.

There was nothing to interest me in his church, a wretched chapel built at the rude Gothic period and even more chilly and uncomfortable than such buildings usually are.

I gave him something for his church, and mounting my mare, I rode back to the château.

I met one of the grooms at the gate, and throwing my bridle to him, walked through the gardens. As I had hoped, I saw the curve of a hooped petticoat on one of the seats, and hurrying towards it found Mademoiselle de Riennes and Mademoiselle Marie seated together, the younger reading her breviary aloud. Her hair caught reflections of gold in the sunlight in a way that enchanted me, and I lost no time in informing her of the fact in terms sufficiently metaphorical to be correct.

My compliments were received with a foolish stare, not even a blush to show they were comprehended. If a woman cannot take a compliment, she is lost. I turned to her sister to be met with better success, while the younger s attention returned to her breviary. Mademoiselle de Riennes tried to distract her from it, fearing, I think, that I might be offended.

'No, no,' replied the fair *dévote*, in an anxious and pleading manner, 'I promised Mother Abbess in Lianon I would always read first. But I will not disturb you by it—I can read elsewhere.'

She was about to rise but I sprang up from the grass where I had been setting at their feet and detained her.

'Do not, I beg of you, Mademoiselle,' said I, 'deprive me of an example as charming as it is edifying. I can never hope to see again such usually opposed qualities in such perfect conjunction.'

Then remembering that I was wasting my breath, I asked her as one would ask a child if she were very fond of the Mother Abbess she mentioned. She did not pay full attention to my question at first and I noticed a habit she continually had of brushing her hand across her eyes and then staring, as though she were not certain of what she saw. Then she answered, 'Oh, yes, very fond. One is safe with her.'

I glanced at Mademoiselle de Riennes to find how she took this odd remark, but was surprised that she seemed to have received it with an unreasonable amount of perturbation. She rallied herself quickly however, and said to me, My sister has always wished to enter the convent at Lianon, which is an order stricter than the convent here at Riennes. She has the vocation.'

I wondered whether Mademoiselle were entirely disinterested, in giving me this information, and I asked her what were her own feelings with regard to the conventual life. She replied in an even tone without a trace of that desire to please that had shown hitherto in all her remarks, 'That it is a useful necessity. That as it is no longer considered humane to expose newly-born daughters to the wolves on the hillside, their parents must be able to place them later in convents where they may die slowly, not from rigours and mortifications but from tedium, the tedium that makes all day and all night seem one perpetual and melancholy afternoon.'

Her eyes glittered with so strange an expression of hatred and even rage, that she, whom I had hitherto considered as the most reasonable of the family, now appeared almost wild. I wondered why her parents had not given her the right of priority which belonged to her, instead of leaving the choice to me.

My father's remarks on the subject came back to me, and I now considered that I had certainly better choose Mademoiselle de Riennes and satisfy the strictest claims of honour and delicacy. This decision was the easier to reach since Mademoiselle Marie had again shown so plainly she was a fool. I rose and took my leave of them that I might go and find the Comte to tell him my decision, for I feared that to wait too long before arriving at it might look like discourtesy.

I walked down an alley between clipped box hedges that rose above my head, and as I turned a corner I saw Mademoiselle Claude walking in my direction. She was correctly attired in a grey lute-string nightgown with ruffles of fine embroidery, her hands were folded in front of her and her head, slightly bent, was neatly dressed. When I had greeted her I asked if she had been walking long in the garden.

'No, Monsieur, she replied, 'I have been to the convent. The chaplain informed me of your pious interest in his church.'

I disliked the thought that the priest I had met was chaplain to the Convent of Riennes—still more, that he had been talking with Mademoiselle Claude. I asked her which of her sisters opinions she shared concerning the religious life—did she not agree with Mademoiselle de Riennes that it was inexpressibly tedious? She smiled very slightly.

'I should not find life in the convent tedious, Monsieur,' she said.

'Then you, like Mademoiselle Marie, have the vocation?'

'I have a vocation.'

As she spoke, she at last raised her eyes and looked up at me, nor did they flicker nor turn away as I looked down into them. It came upon me with a shock, that was not all displeasure, that the eyes of this young girl revealed a deeper knowledge of evil, which is what we generally mean by knowledge of life, than was sounded in all my experience as a travelled man of fashion. And as this struck me, I laughed, in a way that should have frightened her, but only brought her nearer to my side with a low, purring murmur, too soft for a laugh, her eyes still fixed on mine.

An extraordinary sensation swam over me. I was trying to remember something that I had seen in or thought about her eyes the evening before. The effort to remember was so strong that it was like a physical struggle, and though I felt I might succeed if I drew my eyes away from hers for a moment, I could not do this.

Then I noticed that she was humming the tune of the song that she had sung the night before, and as she did so her body rocked a little, backwards and forwards, as though swaying to the measure of a dance, while her eyes never left mine. I advanced a step towards her, she receded, we seemed to be dancing together, though with what steps and movement I could not say. Presently she was speaking to me, chanting the words of the tune—'Monsieur enjoys dancing? Monsieur will dance with me?'

I seized her by the shoulders. She winced and cried out, her lips contorted with pain that my movement, rough as it was, could not have caused by itself. As she tried to pull herself away, her dress slipped over her shoulder and revealed a freshly made scar on the white skin, caused by a knife or some other weapon. I cried out on seeing it and let go of her, but she pulled her dress over it again in an instant, looking back over her shoulder at me and smiling.

'So Monsieur will dance with me,' she said, and moved away from me down the alley so quickly that she seemed to have gone before I had perceived her go.

I was now utterly unwilling to continue my way to the château, to tell the Comte I desired to marry his eldest daughter. I roamed up and down the box alleys for a considerable length of time, ill at ease and dissatisfied. The rest of the day passed in an intolerable mingling of tedium and excitement. I seemed to be waiting for it to pass in eager expectancy of I knew not what. I found myself watching the sun as though I were longing for it to set; again and again I glanced at the clock and told myself, 'The moon will be at the full tonight,' though I did not know what possible interest that could have for me.

I supposed it was some echo of Madame la Comtesses maundering fancies when she had rambled to me about her youngest daughter, and I tried to pull myself up sharply and point out mat I was myself becoming like an old woman, my mind incapable of decision or reasoning, of anything but a feeble repetition of words and phrases that came from

I knew not where.

Yet I could not shake off this mood nor discover what I meant to do regarding my marriage; nor indeed what I was thinking of. I found conversation, even with Mademoiselle de Riennes, unbearably wearisome; it was no pleasure to observe Mademoiselle Marie's beauty which now appeared as insipid and lifeless as a puppet's. I saw Mademoiselle Claude again only in the presence of her parents, but she never spoke nor did she look at me.

In the evening I chanced to be alone with the Comte. I felt that he was expecting me to speak of my marriage, and suddenly I knew that it was only his youngest daughter I had any desire to marry—a desire so burning and importunate that I marvelled I had not realized my wishes sooner. I spoke of them, saying that though I was anxious to perform the part of a man of scrupulous honour, I could not but take advantage of his liberality and make my choice according to the dictates of my heart.

He showed no surprise, and gave his consent in terms appropriate and correct, with nothing that I could interpret as expressive of displeasure. Yet he spoke mechanically and with a strained, uneasy attention, almost, or so it sometimes appeared, as if he were listening and repeating someone else's words, instead of directly answering me. It struck me when he had finished speaking, that he was a smaller and a duller man than I had formerly observed him to be.

I found a pretext for going early to my room, where I paced up and down in a fever of restlessness. In spite of the exaltation of my new desires and the immediate prospect of their fruition, I felt that I had never been so much bored in the course of my whole existence as at that moment; that never before had I discovered how ineffably tedious and wearisome that whole existence had been.

I remembered the various pleasures I had experienced and marvelled that I had ever found zest in them; my deepest passions, my most exciting adventures, now appeared as flat, trivial and insipid as the emotions and escapades of a schoolboy. I wondered with a kind of despair if there were nothing left in life that could amuse me. The fact that my marriage was to be one of inclination should no doubt have answered this question, but I seemed already satiated with that as with all else.

I would have bartered all that was most dear to me, my possessions, my name, my life, my honour, my soul itself, for any new experience that could satisfy this new curiosity and raise me from my intolerable tedium. Desires arose in me so monstrous and unnatural that my thoughts could scarcely find shape or name for them, yet I regarded them calmly, without horror, without even surprise.

At last I went to bed, because however much I longed to

be occupied there was no other occupation for me. In spite of the disordered turmoil in my brain, I fell asleep quickly. No noises disturbed me this time, I did not dream, but I woke as suddenly as I had fallen asleep. I drew back my bed-curtains and saw that the room was full of moonlight, for the window shutters which Jacques had closed before he left me for the night were now wide open, and I could hear a great noise of wind in the pine trees outside. In the middle of the floor stood the white cat, perfectly still, its back arched and tail erect, its pale green eyes glaring at me. It now leaped on to the foot of the bed and began ramping its paws up and down on the quilt in a state of violent excitement, uttering short wild mewing cries.

I kicked it off, but it sprang on to another part of the bed and clawed at the bed-clothes as though trying to pull them off. A cloud must have passed over the moon for the room was momentarily darkened, and a blast of wind came roaring through the pines and rushed in through my open shutters, blowing the bed-curtains all over me, In that instant I could have sworn that I felt the light cold touch of a hand on my heart.

I scrambled out of bed and hurried on my clothes as though my life depended on getting dressed instantly. Clapping on my sword-belt I strode to the door and found the cat there awaiting me. It was purring loudly, and looking back to me if I was following, it trotted into the passage. I could just see a vague shape of something white as it passed before me through the darkness and I followed downstairs and along passages until I came plump against a closed door. I fumbled for bolts and locks and unfastened them, hearing always the purring of the cat close by me. It never occurred to me to wonder why I was following this beast I detested, out of doors in the middle of the night.

As soon as the door was open I hurried out as fast as I could, through the gardens and out on to the countryside. I was not following the cat now, nor did I see it anywhere. I did not know where I was going, but presently I perceived that I was on the same broad slope of moorland where I had ridden that morning. There were sharp risings and fallings in the ground that I had avoided in my ride, and that prevented my seeing far in front; also, though the moon when unclouded shone clear in the sky, a low-lying miasmic fog obscured the ground.

As I rose to the summit of one of these mounds, I stopped and listened. I thought that I had heard music, but as the wind rushed onwards through the pine woods behind me, I could no longer distinguish it. At this moment the whole light of the full moon shone out from behind a hurrying cloud, and I saw vaguely before me in the mist a vast circle of apparently human figures, revolving in furious movement round some huge and dark object of fantastic shape. Clouds of smoke, reddened now and then by fire, rose round this object and were swept onwards in the wind.

I ran towards the circle; as I did so, the music came nearer, now loud, now faint, on the uncertain blast, and I recognized the tune as the same that Mademoiselle Claude had sung to me. I approached cautiously as I drew near. Sometimes the ring of dancers swung so near me that I was within a few feet of them, sometimes it receded far away. All the figures were holding hands and faced outwards, their backs toward the centre of the circle that they formed.

I saw the figures of men, women and even children flying past me; not one had a human face. The faces of goats, toads, cats, of grinning devils and monkeys, showed opposite me for one instant, clear in the moonlight or obscured by the drifting smoke. Those that seemed most horrible of all were white faces that had no features.

Suddenly the ring broke for one instant as it swung within a yard of where I crouched, and at that moment a blinding cloud of smoke blew into my face. A hand was flung out and touched mine, a light cold touch that I knew. I seized it and sprang to my feet, inmediately my other hand was clasped and I was swung madly onwards into the movement of the dance.

I could now no longer see the dancers, not even those on

either side of me whose hands I grasped. I saw nothing but the night, the smoke, the flying landscape, now vague and vast as of an illimitable sea of fog, now black and hideous shapes of mountains that rose sharply in the moonlight. I felt an exhilaration such as I had never known, a brusque and furious enjoyment, as though my senses and powers were quickened beyond their natural limit. Yet again and again I found I was trying to remember something, with the urgency and even the agony that besets one in a nightmare; but my mind appeared to have forsaken its office.

Then without any warning the hands in my clasp were torn from me, and the ring broke in all directions. I staggered back unable to keep my balance in the shock of the suddenly loosened contact; the next instant I realized that she who had first taken my hand had gone, and I was hunting madly for her through that monstrous assembly.

Though the ring had broken, the music continued, and I jostled many who were still dancing, back to back, with their hands joined. In the misty confusion it was impossible to distinguish anything clearly; I thought I saw gigantic toads dressed in green velvet who were carrying dishes, but I did not stay to remark them. Huge clouds of dun-coloured smoke arose before me, lit up momentarily by flames, and in their midst I saw for an instant a shape that seemed greater and more hideous than the human. A mighty voice arose from it, speaking, it seemed, some word of command, and straightaway all the company fell on their knees.

Then I saw her whom I had been seeking. She stood erect on what appeared to be a black throne, the fiery smoke behind her. The moon, darkened of late, shone out on her white limbs that were scarcely concealed by the fluttering rags she wore. Her loosened hair blew straight before her face, and appeared snow-white in the moonlight. Something gleamed in her uplifted hand, she bent, and at this moment an awful cry arose, a sobbing shriek so deformed by its extreme anguish and terror that though it was certainly human I could not distinguish if it were from man, woman or child. The figure rose erect, her arms flung wide as in triumph, her face revealed. It was the face of Mademoiselle Claude.

I rushed towards the throne; it was the huge stone I had observed on my ride. She turned towards me, her face bent down to greet me, her lips parted in laughter, her eyes gleaming as I had never seen them, her whole body transfused with some mysterious force that seemed to fill her with life, pleasure and attraction more than human. My senses reeled as in delirium, I seized her in my arms and dragged her from the stone. In doing so, my hand closed on the knife in hers, and something warm and wet drenched my fingers. The meaning of that hideous death-cry I had just heard suddenly penetrated my numbed and stupefied brain—and I stood stiff with horror, cold sweat breaking out on my hands and forehead.

She twisted herself in my arms till her face looked up into mine; her eyes shone like pale flames and appeared to draw near and then recede very far away, and with them my horror likewise receded until I felt I was forgetting the very cause of it. Yet it seemed to me, as though someone not myself were telling me, that if I did so, the consequences would be worse than death. I struggled desperately to recall what I had felt, and with it something else that all that past day and this night I had been trying to remember. I longed to pray but was ashamed to enlist the aid of a Power that until that moment I had doubted and mocked.

Her arms slid upwards round my neck; my flesh shuddered beneath their embrace as from contact with some loathsome thing, yet she seemed but the more desirable. My consciousness began to fail me as I bent over her. Again the eyes came close, enormous, and I stared at the pupils, black and perpendicular in their green depths. A voice that I did not at first recognize for my own shrieked aloud—'They are not human. Remember, the eyes are not human.'

As I cried out, I found that I could remove my eyes from hers, I looked down at what I held, and on her naked shoulder saw the scar I had observed that morning. I knew now that it had been made by my own sword the night before when I had struck in the darkness at her familiar, and the discovery turned me sick and faint. I frantically repulsed the accursed white body that clung to mine, and made to draw my sword. The witch screamed not in fear but in laughter, and flung herself upon me with her knife before I could get my sword free from its scabbard. I fended off the blow on my heart, and with my left arm dripping blood I seized her wrist while my right, now holding my sword, was raised to strike.

In that instant I was seized from behind by what seemed to be a hundred slippery hands clawing at my neck, arms and ankles. The whole mob, laughing, sobbing, screaming, chuckling, was round me and upon me. It appeared certain that I should be overcome, but I struck out madly with my sword and succeeded in effecting some clearance round me.

A kind of berserker fury consumed me; I rushed upon that obscene herd, striking right and left to hew a passage through them. They fled shrieking in front of me but closed on me from behind; I was bitten, clawed, scratched, hacked at, cut at, with no proper weapons it seemed, but the blows would have been sufficient to overcome me had not all my forces been so desperately engaged.

After a period that seemed to endure for hours, I found mat I was hacking blindly at the empty air; I wiped the blood from my eyes and looking round me saw that I was alone, surrounded only by the mounds and hillocks through which I had approached to that frightful merrymaking. My legs would no longer support me, my senses fled from me, and I fell upon the ground.

I woke to consciousness to see the light of dawn behind the mountains. All was silent; at some distance, a thin column of smoke, as from a dying fire, ascended straight upwards in the still air. I struggled to my feet and with all the strength that was left in my bruised body I dragged myself towards the château.

One of my grooms was in the courtyard as I entered, and cried out on seeing my condition. I cut him short and ordered him to assemble the rest of my band and have my horses saddled with the utmost expedition. I commanded Jacques to leave all my baggage and we were ready for departure, before any of the Comte's household, excepting the servants, were aroused.

In raw and foggy daylight we rode out of the courtyard and down the road that led from Riennes.

I will finish this event in my memories here, though I must traverse six years to do so. The other day, while on a protracted visit to London, I was sitting in White's coffeehouse when Jacques brought me the papers mat I have sent me regularly from France. In one of them was a notice which so much engaged my attention that I lost all account of the conversation around me. My Lord Selborne asked me what news I found so engrossing. I read aloud: In the French Juras a nun, youngest daugnter of the ancient and noble family of R———, has been tried and found guilty of sorcery. She was burnt at the stake. The nun's two sisters are also in the religious life, and the eldest, who is in the same convent, fell under suspicion for some time but has been cleared. In fact so many arrests were made both within the convent and through the whole countryside that it was found impossible to prosecute them all, lest the whole district of R———, the scene of these horrors, should require to be burnt.'

Here my lord interrupted me with expressions of horror that France, even in her remotest provinces, should still be so barbarously superstitious as to bum a woman of quality for a witch.

'In England,' he remarked, 'we got over such whimsies in the time of the Stuarts, and since then the women, God bless 'em, have been allowed to enchant with impunity.'

That very able man, Monsieur Voltaire the playwright, who was then on his visit to England, burst forth in great indignation against the priest-ridden laws of our country that could make such executions possible. What could it matter, he declared, if an ignorant peasantry, rebelling against the tedium of its miserable existence, cared at certain seasons to make a bonfire, dress up one of their number as the Devil, put masks on the rest, and indulge in the mummery of the Witches' Sabbath?

In his grandfather's day, sorcery had been a fashion extending even to the *noblesse* and gentry; the trial of La Voisin, the famous sorceress and prisoner, had implicated hundreds, even, it was whispered, the King's reigning sweetheart, Madame de Montespan herself. Whole villages, indeed whole districts in the Basques and Juras, had been devastated by the laws against witchcraft, and it had proved impossible to deal with all the witches that had been arrested.

'But witchcraft amounted to more than mummery,' declared one Mr. Calthrop. 'On my own estate in my fathers time a stone was thrown at an old woman's dog and the mark was found on *her* body.'

Monsieur Voltaire waved this aside. He had heard many such instances and did not deny that there was foundation for them. Such people as believed themselves to be witches were certainly abnormal, and they, and the animals they used as their ministers, might well have abnormal powers. But he was certain that the world did not yet fully realize the powers of thought and belief. He considered it possible that future ages would attribute such instances of unnatural sympathy between a witch and her familiars to an unnatural state of mind and body. He addressed his remarks chiefly to me, but I did not answer them.

In spite of the fact that as I am now approaching my thirty-first year, middle age is hard upon me, I have still to find a wife to carry on my family.

THE WITCH CHARMER

'*I will relate to you some examples, which I have gained in part from the teachers of our faculty, in part from the experience of a certain upright secular judge, worthy of all faith, who from the torture and confessions of witches and from his experiences in public and private has learned many things of this sort—a man with whom I have often discussed this subject broadly and deeply—to wit, Peter, a citizen of Berne, in the diocese of Lausanne, who has burned many witches of both sexes, and has driven others out of the territory of the Bernese. I have moreover conferred with one Benedict, a monk of the Benedictine order, who, although now a very devout cleric in a reformed monastery at Vienna, was a decade ago, while still in the world, a necromancer, juggler, buffoon, and strolling player, well known as the delight of village children everywhere.*

From the 15th century *Formicarius* of Johannes Nider, the Dominican theologian who provided the clue that magic might form the basis of one of the most famous of all German legends. . . .

*Duke of Orleans, Regent of France during the minority of Louis XV. *Anne of Austria, mother of Louis XIV and Regent of France during his minority. *Louis XV.

THE DREAM CIRCEAN

ALEISTER CROWLEY

I

Perched at the junction of two of the steepest little streets in Montmartre shines the 'Lapin Agile,' a tiny window filled with gleaming bottles, thrilled through by the light behind, a little terrace with tables, chairs and shrubs, and two dark doors.

Roderic Mason came striding up the steepness of the Rue St. Vincent, his pipe gripped hard in his jaw; for the hill is too abrupt for lounging. On the terrace he stretched himself, twirled round half a dozen times like a dervish, pocketed his pipe, and went stooping through the open doorway.

Grand old Frédéric was there, in his Vast corduroys and sou'wester hat, a cello in his hand.

His trim grey beard was a shade whiter than when Roderic bad last patronized the 'Lapin,' five years before; but the kindly, gay, triumphant eyes were nowise dimmed by time. He knew Roderic at a glance, and gave his left hand carelessly, as if he had been gone but yesterday. Time ambles easily for

103

the owner of such an eyrie, his life content with wine and song and simple happiness.

It is in such as Frédéric that the hope of the world lies. You could not bribe Frédéric with a motor-car to grind in an office and help to starve and enslave his fellows. The bloated, short-of-breath, bedizened magnates of commerce and finance are not life, but a disease. The monster hotel is not hospitality, but imprisonment. Civilization is a madness; and while there are men like Frédéric there is a hope that it will pass. Woe to the earth when Bumble and Rockefeller and their victims are the sole economic types of man!

Roderic sat down on his favourite bench against the wall, and took stock of things.

How well he remembered the immense Christ at the end of the room, a figure conceived by a giant of old time, one might have thought, and now covered with a dry, green lichenous rot, so that the limbs were swollen and distorted. It gave an incredibly strong impression of loathsome disease, entirely overpowering the intention of picturing inflicted pain.

Roderic, who, far from being a good man, was actually a Freethinker, thought it a grimly apt symbol of the religion of our day.

On His right stood a plaster Muse, with a lvre, the effect being decidedly improved by someone who had affixed a comic mask with a grinning mouth and a long pink nose; on His left a stone plaque of Lakshmi, the Hindu Venus, a really very fine piece of work, clean and dignified, in a way the one sanity in the room, except for an exquisite pencil sketch of a child, done with all the delicacy and strength of Whistler. The rest of the decoration was a delicious mixture of the grotesque and the obscene. Sketches, pastels, cuts, cartoons, oils, all the media of art, had been exhausted in a noble attempt to flagellate impurity—impurity of thought, line, colour, all we symbolize by womanhood.

Hence the grotesque obscenity in nowise suggested Jewry; but gave a wholesome reaction of life and youth against artificiality and money-lust.

As it chanced, there was nobody of importance in the 'Lapin.' Frédéric, with his hearty voice and his virile roll, more of a dance than a walk, easily dominated the company.

Yet there was at least one really remarkable figure in the pleasant gloom of the little cabaret.

A man sat there, timid, pathetic, one would say a man often rebuffed. He was nigh seventy years of age, maybe; he looked older. For him time had not moved at all, apparently; for he wore the dress of a beau of the Second Empire.

Exquisitely, too, he wore it. Sitting back in his dark corner, the figure would have gained had it been suddenly transplanted to the glare of a state ball and the steps of a throne.

Merrily Frédéric trolled out an easy, simple song with the perfect art—how different from the laborious inefficiency of the Opera!—and came over to Roderic to see that his coffee was to his liking.

'Changes, Frédéric,!' he said, a little sadly. 'Where is Madeleine la Vache?'

'At Lourcine.'

'Mimi l'Engeuleuse?'

'At Clamart.'

'The Scotch Count, who always spoke like a hanging judge?'

'Went to Scotland—he could get no more whisky here on credit.'

'His wife?'

'Poor girl! poor girl!'

'Ah! it was bound to happen. And Bubu Tire-Cravat?'

Frédéric brought the edge of his hand down smartly on the table, with a laugh.

'He had made so many widows, it was only fair he should marry one!' commented the Englishman. And Pea-shooter Charley?'

'Don't know. I think he is in prison in England.'

'Well, well; it saddens. "Where are the snows of yesteryear?" I must have an absinthe; I feel old.'

'You are half my years,' answered Frédéric. 'But come! If yesteryear be past, it is this year now. And all these distinguished persons who are gone, together are not worth one silver shoe-buckle of yonder—' Frédéric nodded towards the old beau.

'True, I never knew him; yet he looks as if he had sat there since Sedan. Who is he?'

'We do not know his name, monsieur,' said Frédéric softly, a little awed; 'but I think he was a duke, a prince—I cannot say what. He is more than that—he is unique. He is—*le Revenant de la Rue des Quatre Vents*!'

'The Ghost of the Street of the Four Winds,' Roderic was immensely taken by the title; a thousand fantastic bases for the sobriquet jumped into his brain. Was the Rue des Quatre Vents haunted by a ghost in his image? There are no ghosts in practical Paris. But of all the ideas whicn came to him, not one was half so strange as the simple and natural story which he was later to hear.

'Come,' said Frédéric. 'I will present you to him.'

'Monseigneur,' he said, as Roderic stood before him, ready to make his little bow, 'let me present Monsieur Mason, an Englishman.'

The old fellow took no notice. Said Frédéric in his ear: 'Monsieur lives on the Boulevard St. Germain, and loves to paint the streets.'

The old man rose with alacrity, smiled, bowed, was enchanted to meet one of the gallant allies whose courage had—he spoke glibly of the Alma, Inkerman, Sebastopol.

The little comedy had not been lost on Roderic. Wondering, he sat down beside the old nobleman.

What spell had Frédéric wrought of so potent a complexion?

'Sir,' he said, 'the gallantly of the French troops at the Malakoff was beyond all praise; it will live for ever in history.'

To another he might have spoken of the *entente cordiale;* to this man he dared not.

Had not his brain perhaps stopped in the sixties?

Had the catastrophe of '70 broken his heart?

Roderic must walk warily.

But the conversation did not take the expected turn. The old gentleman elegantly, wittily, almost gaily, chattered of art, of music, of the changed appearance of Paris. Here, at any rate, he was *au courant des affaires.*

Yet as Roderic, puzzled and pleased, finished his absinthe he said more seriously than he had yet spoken: 'I hear that monsieur is a great painter (Roderic modestly waved aside the adjective), 'has painted many pictures of Paris. Indeed, as I think of it, I seem to remember a large picture of St. Sulpice at the Salon of eight years ago—no, seven years ago.'

Roderic stared in surprise. How should any one—such a man, of all men—remember his daub, a thing he himself had long forgotten? The oldster read his thought. 'There was one corner of that picture which interested me deeply, deeply,' he said. 'I called to see you; you had gone—none knew where. I am indeed glad to have met you at last. Perhaps you would be good enough to show me your pictures—you have other pictures of Paris? I am interested in Paris—in Paris itself—in the stones and bricks of it. Might I—if you have nothing better to do—come to your studio now, and see them?'

'I'm afraid the light—' began Roderic. It was now ten o'clock.

'That is nothing, returned the other. 'I have my own criteria of excellence. A match-glimmer serves me.'

There was only one explanation of all this. The man must be an architect, perhaps ruined in the mad speculations of the Empire, so well described by Zola in *La Curée*.

'At your service, sir,' he said, and rose. The old fellow was surely eccentric; but equally he was not dangerous. He was rich, or he would not be wearing a diamond worth every penny of two thousand pounds, as Roderic, no bad judge, made out. There might be profit, and there would assuredly be pleasure.

They waved, the one an airy, the other a courteous, goodnight to grand old Frédéric, and went out.

The old man was nimble as a kitten; he had all the suppleness of youth; and together they ran rapidly down to the boulevard, where, hailing a fiacre, they jumped in and clattered down towards the Seine.

Roderic sat well back in the carriage, a little lost in thought. But the old man sat upright, and peered eagerly about him. Once he stopped the cab suddenly at a house with a low railing in front of it, well set back from the street, jumped out, examined it minutely, and then, with a sigh and a shake of the head, came back, a little wearier, a little older.

They crossed the Seine, rattled up the Rue Bonaparte, and stopped at the door of Roderic's studio.

II

'Ah, well, said the old man, as he concluded his examination of the pictures, 'What I seek is not here. If it will not weary you, I will tell you a story. Perhaps, although you have not painted it, you have seen it. Perhaps—bah! I am seventy years of age, and a fool to the end.

'Listen, my young friend! I was not always seventy years of age, and that of which I have to tell you happened when I was twenty-two.

'In those days I was very rich, and very happy. I had never loved; I cared for nobody. My parents were both dead long since. A year of freedom from the control of my good old guardian, the Duc de Castelnaudary (God rest his soul!), had left me yet taintless as a flower. I had that chivalrous devotion to woman which perhaps never really existed at any time save for rare individuals.

'Such a one is ripe for adventure, and since, as your great poet has said, "Circumstance bows before those who never miss a chance," it was perhaps only a matter of time before I met with one.

'Indeed (I will tell you, for it will help you to understand my story), I once found myself in an extremely absurd position through my fantastic trust in the impeccability of woman.

'It was rather late one night, and I was walking home

through a deserted street, when two brutal-looking ruffians came towards me, between them a young and beautiful girl, her face flushed with shame, and screaming in pain; for the savages had each firm hold of one arm, and were forcing her at a rapid pace—to what vile den?

'My fist in the face of one and my foot in the stomach of the other! They sprawled in the road, and, disdaining them, I turned my back and offered my arm to the girl. She, in an excess of gratitude, flung her arms round my neck and began to kiss me furiously—the first kiss I had ever had from a woman, mind you! Maybe I would not have been altogether displeased, but that she stank so foully of brandy that—my gorge rises at the memory. The ruffians, more surprised than hurt, began laughing, but kept well away. I tried to induce the girl to come home; in the end she lost her temper, and fell to belabouring me with her fists. I was not strong enough or experienced enough to contend with a madwoman, and I could not allow myself to strike her. She beat me sore. . . .

'I can remember the scene now as if it were yesterday: the bewildered boy, the screaming, swearing, kicking, scratching woman, the two "savages" (honest *bourgeois* enough!) reeling against the houses, crying with laughter, too weak with laughter to stand straight.

'By-and-by they took pity, came forward, and released me from the unpleasant situation.

'But the shame of me, as I slunk away down the streets! I would not go home that night at all, ashamed to face my own servants.

'I told myself, in the end, that this was a rare accident; but for all that there must have remained a slight stain upon the mirror of perfect chivalry. In the old days when they taught logic in the schools one learnt how delicate a flower was a "universal affirmative."'

'It was some uneventful months after this "tragedy of the ideal" that I was again walking home very late. I had been to the Jardin des Plantes in the afternoon, and, dining in that quarter, had stayed lingering on the bridge watching the Seine. The moon dropped down behind the houses—with a start I realized that I must go home. There was some danger, you understand, of footpads. Nothing, however, occurred until—I always preferred to walk through the narrow streets; there is romance in narrow streets!—I found myself in the Rue des Quatre Vents; not a stone's-throw from this house, as you know.

'I had been thinking of my previous misadventure, and, with the folly of youth, had been indulging in a reverie of the kind that begins "If only." If only she had been a princess ravished by a wicked ogre. If only . . . If only . . .

'On the south side of the Rue des Quatre Vents is a house standing well back from the street, with a railing in front of it—a common type, is it not? But what riveted my attention upon it was that while the front of the house was otherwise entirely dark, from a window on the first floor streamed a blaze of light. The window was wide open to the street; voices came from it.

'The first an old, harsh, menacing voice, with all the sting of hate in it; nay, the sting of something devilish, worse than hate. A corrupt enjoyment of its malice informed it. And the words it spoke were too infamous for me to repeat. They are scarred upon my brain. Addressed to the vilest harridan that scours the gutter for her carrion prey, they would have yet been inhuman, impossible; to the voice that answered . . . !

'It was a voice like the tinkling of a fairy bell. Whoever spoke was little more than a child; and her answer had the purity and strength of an angel. That even the foul monster who addressed her could support it, unblasted, was matter for astonishment.

'Now the older voice broke into filthy insult, a very frenzy of malice.

'I heard—O God!—the swish of a whip, and the sound of it falling upon flesh.

'There was silence, awhile, save for the hideous laughter of the invisible horror inside.

'At last a piteous little moan.

'My blood sang shrill within me. Out of myself, I sprang

at the railings, and was over them in a second. Rapidly, and quite unobserved (for the scene was strenuous within), I climbed up the grating of the lower windows, and, reaching up to the edge of the balcony, swung myself up to and over it.

'As I stopped to fetch breath, as yet unperceived, I took in the scene, and was staggered at its strangeness.

'The room, though exquisitely decorated, was entirely bare of furniture, unless one could dignify by that name a heap of dirty straw in one corner, by which stood a flattish wooden bowl, half full of what looked like a crust of bread mashed into pulp with water.

'Half turned away from me stood the owner of the harsh voice and soul abominable. It was a woman of perhaps sixty years of age, the head of an angel—so regular were the features, so silver-white the hair—set upon the deformed body of a dwarf. Hairy hands and twisted arms, a hunched back and bandy legs; in the gnarled right hand a terrible whip, the carved jade handle blossoming into a rose of fine cords, shining with silver—sharp, three-cornered chips of silver! The whole dripped black with blood. Upon the angel face stood a sneer, a snarl, a malediction. The effect upon one's sense of something beyond the ordinary was, too, heightened by her costume; for though the summer was at its height she was clad from head to foot in ermine, starred, more heavily than is usual, with the little black tails in the form of *fleurs-de-lis*.

'In extreme contrast to this monster was a young girl crouching upon the floor. At first sight one would have hardly suspected a human form at all, for from her head flowed down on all sides a torrent of exquisite blonde gold, that completely hid her. Only two little hands looked out, clasped, pleading for mercy, and a fairy child-face looking up—in vain—to that black heart of hatred. Even as I gazed the woman hissed out so frightful a menace that my blood ran chill. The child shrank back into herself. The other raised her whip. I leapt into the room. The old hag spat one infamous word at me, turned on me with the whip.

'This time I was under no illusions about the sanctity of womanhood. With a single blow I felled her to the ground. My signet-ring cut her lip, and the blood trickled over her cheek. I laughed. But the child never moved—it would seem she hardly comprehended.

'I turned, bowed. "I could not bear to hear your cries," I said—rather obviously, one may admit. "I came—" adding under my breath, "I saw, I conquered." "Who is that?" I added sternly, pointing to the prostrate hag.

' "Ah, sir" (she began to cry), "it is my mother." The horror of it was tenfold multiplied. "She—she—" The child blushed, stammered, stopped.

' "I heard, mademoiselle," I cried indignantly.

' "I am here" (she sobbed) "for a month, starved, whipped—oh! By day the window barred with iron; by night, open, the more to mock my helplessness!" Then, with a sudden cry, her little pink hand darting out and showing a faultless arm: "Look! look! she is on you."

'The mother had drawn herself away with infinite stealth, regained her feet, and, a thin stiletto in her hand, was crouched to spring. Indeed, as she leapt I was hard put to it to avoid the lunge; the dagger-edge grazed my arm as I stepped aside.

'I turned. She was on me, flinging me aside with the force of her rush as if I had been a straw. The snarl of her was like a wolf.

'This time she cut me deep. Again a whirl, a rush. I altered my tactics; I ran in to meet her. Hampered as she was by her furs, I was now quicker than she. I struck her dagger arm so strongly that the blade flew into the air, and fell quivering on the floor, the heavy hilt driving the thin blade deep into the polished wood. Even so I had her by the waist, catching her arm, and with one heave of my back I tossed her into the air, careless where she might fall.

'As luck would have it, she struck the balcony rail, broke it, and fell upon the pavement of the court. There was a crash, but no cry, no groan. I went to the balcony. She lay still, as the living do not lie, and her white hair was blackening, lapped by a congealing stream.

'I withdrew into the room. Since I have learnt that any death brings with it a strange sense of relief. There is a certain finality. *La comédie est jouée*—and one turns with new life to the next business.

'The golden child had never stirred. But now she crouched lower, and fell to soft, sweet crying.

' "Your mother is dead," I said abruptly. "May I offer you the guardianship of my godmother, the Duchess of Castelnaudary? Come, mademoiselle, let us go."

' "I thank you, sir," she answered, still sobbing; "but Jean is awake and at the door. Jean is fierce and lean as an old wolf."

'I pulled the dagger from the floor. "I am fierce and lithe as a young lion!" I said. "Let the old wolf beware!"

' "But I cannot, sir, I cannot. I. . . ." Her confusion became acute.

' "I dare not move, sir—I—I—my mother has taken away all my clothes."

'I marvelled. In her palace of gold hair nobody could have guessed it. But now I blushed, and lively. The dilemma was absurd.

' "I have it," said I. "I will climb down and bring up the ermine."

'She shuddered at the idea. Her dead mother s furs!

' "It must be," I said firmly.

' "Go, brave knight!'—a delicate smile lit up her face—"I trust myself to you."

'I bent on my right knee to her. "I take you," I said, "to be my lady, to fight in your cause, to honour and love you for ever."

'She put out her right hand—oh, the delicate beauty of it! I kissed it. "My knight," she said, "Jean is below; he may hear you; you go perhaps to your death—kiss me!"

'With a sob I sought her once full in my arms, and our mouths met. I closed my eyes in trance; my muscles failed; I sank, my forehead to the ground before her.

'When I opened my eyes again she too was praying. Softly, without a word, I stepped to the window, took the dagger in my teeth, dropped from the edge, landed lightly beside the corpse. She was quite dead, the skull broken in, the teeth exposed in a last snarl. She lay on her back; I opened the coat, turned her over. The gruesome task was nearly finished when the door of the house opened, and an old man, his face scarred, one lip cut half away in some old brawl, so that he grinned horribly and askew, rushed out at me, a rapier in his hand. My stiletto, though long beyond the ordinary, was useless against a tool of such superior reach.

'A last wrench gave me the ermine cloak, an invaluable

parry. Could I entangle his sword, he was at my mercy. He saw it, and fenced warily. Indeed, I had the upper hand throughout. Threatening to throw the cloak, catch his sword, blind him, rush in with my dagger—he gave back and back in a circle round the courtyard.

'No sound came from the room above. Probably we three were alone. The fight was not to be prolonged for ever; the weight of the fur would tire me soon, counter-balance the advantage of age. Then, almost before I knew what had happened, we were fighting in the street. I would not cry for help; one was more likely to rouse a bandit than a guardian of the peace. And, besides, who could say how the law stood?

'I had certainly killed a lady; I was doing my best, with the aid of her stolen cloak, to kill a servant of the house; I contemplated an abduction. Best kill him silently, and be gone.

'But when and how had Jean pulled open the iron gates and retreated into the street?

'It mattered little, though certainly it left an uneasy sense of bewilderment; what mattered was that here we were fighting in semi-darkness—the dawn was not fairly lifted— for life and death.

' "Ten thousand crowns, Monsieur Jean," I cried, "and my service!"—I gave him my style—"I see you can be a faithful servant."

' "Faithful to death!" he retorted, and I was sorry to have to kill him.

'We fenced grimlv on.

' "But," I urged, "your mistress is dead. Your duty is to her child, and I am her child's—"

'He looked up from my eyes. "An omen!" he cried, pointing to the great statue of St. Michael trampling Satan, for we had come fighting to the Place St. Michel. "Darkness yields to light; I am your servant, sir." He dropped on one knee, and tendered the hilt of his sword.

'But as I put out my hand to take it (guarded against attack, I boast me, but not against the extraordinary trick which followed) he suddenly snatched at the ermine, which lay loosely on my left arm, and, leaving me with sword and dagger, fled with a shriek of laughter across the Place St. Michel, and, flinging the furs over the bridge, himself plunged into the Seine and swam strongly for the other bank.

'There was no object in pursuing him; I would recover the furs, and return triumphant. Alas! they had sunk; they were now whirled far away by the swift river. Where should I get a cloak?

'How stupid of me! The old woman had plenty of other clothes beneath her furs; I would take them.

'And I set myself gaily to run back to the house.

III

'Whether by excitement I took the wrong turning, or whether—but you will hear!—in short, I do not clearly understand even now why I did not at once find the road. But at least I did fail to find it, discovered, as I supposed, my error, corrected it, failed once more. . . . In the end I got flustered—so much hung on my speedy return!—I fluttered hither and thither like a wild pigeon whose mate has been shot. I stopped short, pulled myself together. Let me think it out! Where am I now? I was under the shadow (the dawn just lit its edge) of the mighty shoulder of St. Sulpice. "More haste, less speed!" I said to myself. "I will walk deliberately down to the boulevard, turn east, and so I cannot possibly miss the Carrefour de l'Odéon"—out of which, as I knew of old, the Rue des Quatre Vents leads. Indeed, I remembered the carrefour from that night. I had passed through it. I remembered hesitating as to which turning to take. For, as you know, the carrefour is a triangle, one road leading from the apex, four (with two minor variations just off the carrefour) from the base.

'Following this plan, I came, sure enough, in three minutes or so into the Rue des Quatre Vents. It is not a long street, as you know, and I thought that I remembered perfectly that the house faced the tiny Rue St. Grégoire, which leads back to the Boulevard St. Germain. Indeed, it was down that obscure alley that Jean and I had gone in our fight. I remembered how I had expected to meet somebody on issuing into the boulevard; and then . . . I must have been very busv fighting: I could not remember anything at all of the fight between that issue and the place of Jean's feint and flight.

'Well, here I was: the house should have been in front of me—and it was not. I walked up and down the street; there was no house of the kind, no railings. No residential house. Yet I could not believe myself mistaken. I pinched myself; I was awake. Further, the pinching demonstrated the existence of a sword and dagger in my hands. I was bleeding, too; my left arm twice grazed. I took out my watch; four o'clock. Since I left the bridge—ah! when had I left the bridge? I could not tell—yes, I could. At moon-set. The moon was nine days old.

'No; everything was real. I examined the sword and the stiletto. Silver-gilt; blades of exquisite fineness; the cipher of a princely house of France shone in tiny diamonds upon the pommels.

'The thought sent new courage and determination thrilling through me. I had saved a princess from shame and torture; I loved her! She loved me, for I had saved her—ah! but I had not yet saved her. That was to do.

'But how to act? I had plenty of time. Jean would not

return to the house, in all probability. But the markets were stirring; the weapons and my blood would arouse curiosity. Well, how to act?

'The positive certitude that I had had about the name of the street was my bane. Had I doubted I could have more easily carried out the systematic search that I proposed. But as it was my organized patrol of the quarter was not scientific; I was biased. I came back again and again to the street and searched it, as if the house might nave been hidden in the gutter or vanished and reappeared by magic; as if my previous search might (by some incredible chance) have been imperfect, through relaxed attention. So one may watch a conjuror, observing every movement perfectly, except the one flash which does the trick.

'The search, too, could not be long; so I reflected as disappointment sobered me. One cannot go far from the Carrefour de l'Odéon in any direction without striking some unmistakable object. The two boulevards, the schools, the Odéon itself, St. Sulpice—one could not be far off. Yet—could I possibly have mistaken the Odéon for the Luxembourg?

'Could I . . . ? . . . ? A host of conjectures chased each other through my brain, bewildering it, leading the will to falter, the steps to halt.

'Beneath, keener anguish than the thrust of a poisoned

rapier, stabbed me this poignant pang: my love awaits me, waits for me to save her, to fly with her. . . .

'Where was she?

'It was broad day; I cleansed myself of the marks of battle, sat down and broke my fast, my sane mind steadily forcing itself to a sober plan of action, beating manfully down the scream of its despair. All day I searched the streets. Passing an antiquary, I showed him my weapons. He readily supplied their history; but—there was none of that family alive, nor had been since the great Revolution. Their goods? The four winds of heaven might know. At those words "the four winds" I rushed out of the shop, as if stung by an adder.

'I drove home, set all my servants hunting for railed houses. They were to report to me in the Rue des Quatre Vents. Any house not accounted for, any that might conceal a mystery, these I would see myself.

'All labour lost! My servants tried. I distrusted their energy: I set myself obstinately to scour Paris.

'There is a rule of mathematics which enables one to traverse completely any labyrinth. I applied this to the city. I walked in every road of it, marking the streets at each comer as I passed with my private seal. Each railed house I investigated separately and thoroughly. By virtue of my position I was welcome everywhere. But every night I paced the Rue des Quatre Vents, awaiting . . .

'Awaiting what? Well, in the end, perhaps death. The children gibed at me; passers-by shunned me.

' *"Le Revenant,"* they whispered, *"de la Rue des Quatre Vents."*

'I had forgot to tell you one thing which most steadfastly confirmed me in the search. Two days after the adventure I passed, hot on the quest, by the Morgue. Two women came out. "Not pretty, the fish!" said one. "He with the scarred lip—"

'I heard no more, ran in. There on the slab, grinning yet in death, was Jean. His swim had ended him. Faithful to death!

'I watched long. I offered a huge sum for his identification. The authorities even became suspicious: why was I so anxious? How could I say? He was the servant of . . .

'I did not know my sweet child's name!

'So, while a living man, I made myself a ghost.

IV

'It may have been one day some ten years later,' continued the old nobleman, when as I paced uselessly the Street of the Four Winds I was confronted by a stem, grey figure, short, stout, and bearded, but of an indescribable majesty and force.

'He laid his hand unhesitatingly upon my shoulder. "Unhappy man!" he cried, "thou art sacrificing thy life to a phantom. 'Look not,' quoth Zoroaster, 'upon the Visible Image of the Soul of Nature, for Her name is Fatality.' What thou hast seen—I know not what it is, save that it is as a dog-faced demon that seduceth thy soul from the sacred Mysteries; the Mysteries of Life and Duty."

' "Let me tell my story!" I replied, "and you shall judge—for, whoever you may be, I feel your power and truth."

' "I am Eliphaz Levi Zahed—men call me the Abbé Constant," returned the other.

' "The great magician?"

' "The enemy of the great magician."

'We went together to my house. I had begun to suspect some trick of Hell. The malice of that devilish old woman, it might be, had not slept, even at her death. Had she hidden the house beneath a magic veil? Or had her death itself in some strange way operated to—to what? Even conjecture paled.

127

'But magic somewhere there must be, and Eliphaz Levi was the most famous adept in Paris at the time.

'I told my story, just as I have told it to you, but with strong passion.

' "There is an illusion, master!" I ended. "Put forth the power, and destroy it!"

' "Were I to destroy the illusion," returned the magus, "thinkest thou to see a virgin with gold hair? Nay, but the Eternal Virgin, and a Gold that is not gold."

' "Is nothing to be done?"

' "Nothing!" he replied, with a strange light in his eyes. "Yet, in order to be able to do nothing, thou must first accomplish everything.

' "One day," he smiled, seeing my bewilderment, "thou wilt be angry with the fool who proffers such a platitude."

'I asked him to accept me as a pupil.

' "I require pay," he answered, "and an oath."

' "Speak; I am rich."

' "Every Good Friday," said the adept, "take thirty silver crowns and offer them to the Hospital for the Insane."

' "It shall be done," I said.

' "Swear, then," he went on, "swear, then, here to me"—he rose, terrible and menacing—"by Him that sitteth upon the Holy Throne and liveth and reigneth for ever and ever, that never again, neither to save life, nor to retain honour, wilt thou set foot in the Street of the Four Winds; so long as life shall last."

'Even as he bade me, I rose with lifted hand and swore.

'As I did so there resounded in the room ten sharp knocks, as of ivory on wood, in a certain peculiar cadence.

'This was but the first of a very large number of interviews. I sought, indeed, steadfastly to learn from him the occult wisdom of which he was a master; but, though he supplied me with all conceivable channels of knowledge—books, manuscripts, papyri—yet all these were lifeless; the currents of living water flowed not through them. Should one say that the master withheld initiation, or that the pupil failed to obtain it?

'But at least time abated the monomania—for I know now that my whole adventure was but a very vivid dream, an insanity of adolescence. At this moment I would not like to say at what point exactly in the story fact and dream touch; I have still the sword and dagger. Is it possible that in a trance I actually went through some other series of adventures than that I am conscious of? May not Jean have been a thief, whom I dispossessed of his booty? Had I done this unconsciously it would account for both the weapons and the scene in the Morgue. . . . But I cannot say.

'So, too, I learnt from the master that all this veil of life is but a shadow of a vast reality beyond, perceptible only to those who have earned eyes to see withal.

'These eyes I could not earn; a faith in the master sustained me. I began to understand, too, a little about the human brain; of what it is capable. Of Heaven—and of Hell!

'Life passed, vigorous and pleasant; the only memory that haunted me was the compulsion of my oath that never would I again set foot in the Rue des Quatre Vents.

'Life passed, and for the master ended. "The Veil of the Temple is but a Spiders web!" he said, three days before he died. I followed Eliphaz Levi Zahed to the grave.

'I could not follow him beyond.

'For the next year I applied myself with renewed vigour to the study of the many manuscripts which he had left me. No result could I obtain; I slackened. Followed the folly of my life: I rationalized.

'Thus: one day, leaning over the Pont St. Michel, I let the whole strange story flow back through my brain. I remembered my agony; my present calm astonished me. I thought of Levi, of my oath. "He did not mean *for all my life*," I thought; "he meant until I could contemplate the affair without passion. Is not fear failure? I will walk through just once, to show my mastery." In five minutes—with just one inward qualm—again I was treading the well-worn flags of that ensorcelled road.

'Instantly—instantly!—the old delusion had me by the

throat. I had broken my oath; I was paying the penalty.

'Crazier than ever, I again sought throughout changed Paris for my dream-love; I shall seek her till I die. If I seem calmer, it is but that age has robbed me of the force of passion. In vain you tell me, laughing, that if she ever lived, she is long since dead; or at least is an old woman, the blonde gold faded, the child-face wrinkled, the body bowed and lax. I laugh at you—at you—for a blaspheming ass. Your folly is too wild to anger me!'

'I did not laugh,' said Roderic gravely.

'Well,' said the old man, rising, 'I fear I have wearied you. . . . I thank you for your patience. . . . I know I am a mad old fellow. But, if you should happen—you know. Please communicate. Here is my card. I must go now. I am expected elsewhere. I am expected.'

BLACK MAGIC SOCIETIES

'Rumours that Black Magic Secret Societies exist in London have long been current. It was in Chelsea that I first met dabblers in the Black Art, among them Aleister Crowley, in whose studio I saw a ritual ceremony. It was a trifle spectacular and dramatic, but none the less harmless to all concerned; whereas what I have seen and heard elsewhere, not only in London, but in Paris and New York, has not always been harmless. I have seen things that have horrified and disgusted me and proved to me that there is a great power of evil abroad in the modern world.'

ELLIOTT T. O'DONNELL,

Secret Cults and Secret Societies of Modern London

THE PRIMATE OF THE ROSE

M. P. SHIEL

' "Friends of the Rose?" ' said E. P. Crooks to Smyth one night, at the Savage Club. 'Is it an actual fact that there are secret societies in London?'

And Smyth, with his expression of lazy surprise, replied: 'Why, yes. Ask me another time. Come and dine with us too, if you like:'

It is a wonder that Crichton Smyth ever did invite Crooks. As editor of the *Westminster Magazine*, he had known Crooks as a little story-writer, and had never had any such impulse; but suddenly Englishmen, with their genius for discovery, had discovered that they had a Crooks; proceeded to pay him ninepence for writing 'the'; and then Smyth, with his eyebrows of surprise, muttered: 'Come and dine with us.'

Smyth was of that better aristocracy, the upper middle-class, which gives to England its ladies: slim, clean-looking, old-blooded—not much blood, and thin: but rare, like wine of Yquem.

Of another family was Crooks—a fatty little man, fat-cheeked, with an outsticking moustache that hung. Still, there was something or other in him—something brisk in his glance, in the dash of his hair across his forehead; and if at seventeen he had vended soda-water from door to door, at twenty-six he was a graduate, and at thirty-six a star.

But he was a gay Romeo, Crooks—in a rather vulgar mood; and Smyth had a sister.

If one had prophesied to Smyth that his sister, Minna Smyth of the Smyths, could possible commit follies for E. P. Crooks, or look twice at Crooks, Smyth would hardly have bothered to smile. . . .

However, the human female can be pretty queer and wayward; and her heart is like spittle on the palm that the Tartar slaps—no telling which way it will pitch.

From that first night of the dinner Minna Smyth showed herself amiable to the celebrity—a *chic* dinner of dated wines in a flat in Westminster: for editors are awfully well-to-do people—do you know? The piano there was a mosaiced thing in mother-of-pearl; and, in turning Miss Smyths music, Crooks's fingers got positive magnetism, hers negative, and they met.

She was a tall, thin girl of twenty-five, very like Smyth, very English in type, pretty, but washed-out and superfine, with light eyes of the colour of quinine-solution which X-rays make 'fluorescent.' Was Crooks genuinely smitten with this? It is doubtful. Besides, he was married. But she was a conquest worth making, and he was a man ever on the *qui vive* to add yet a photo to his packet, and a feather to his cap.

Minna Smyth, for her part, took studiously from that night to feeding her mind on the spiced meat of Crooks's books, who, meanwhile, had retaliated upon Smyth by banqueting him at the National Liberal, and might drive home anon with him from the Savage, Crooks felt that he was patronizing Smyth; and Smyth felt that he was patronizing Crooks: for when one has known a tremendous man in his days of '£2-a-thousand-words,' one has no respect for his tremendousness—especially Smyth, who was the chilliest thing that the Heavens ever invented. At any rate, they became friendly.

During which time Crooks and Minna Smyth had a way of meeting at private views, lectures, concerts—meetings of which Smyth did not know; letters were written which Smyth did not see; and it happened one evening at the flat, at a moment when Smyth was in the next room, that Minna mentioned to Crooks in the course of conversation that on Friday nights her brother was out 'at his secret society,' and never came home till 4 a.m.

On this Crooks, picking up her hand, said to her: 'I'll come on Friday night.'

She looked at him under her eyes, meditating upon him; then moved her face from side to side, while her lips took the shape of 'No.'

'Something to *say*,' said he 'I hope you are inexorable.'

Her lids now veiled her eyes, while her bosom rose and rose, unloaded itself of a sigh, and tumbled back.

'Is it yes?'he whispered.

'*Crichton!*' she breathed, with a sudden expression of shrinking and fright in her eyes.

'Oh, I think that that will be all right about Crichton,' Crooks said.

'You don't *know* him!' she whispered: 'his nose goes white. . . .'

Smyth now came in; and presently, when Minna had gone out, Crooks said to him: 'By the way, how about that wondrous "Friends of the Rose," Smyth, that you are always to tell me of?' He threw himself into roomy red velvet opposite Smyth's red velvet on the other side of a fire—it was December—and drank from a large and fragile glass.

'What can one tell of it, if it is a secret society?' Smyth asked, his eyebrows raised over lazy lids that seemed to strain to be open, for there was an ample valley of country between his eyebrows and his nose-tip.

'I mean to say—is the thing *real?* Is it like *London?*'—from Crooks, who had an inquisitive intellect, and, then, was ever on the quest of 'copy.' He added: 'Years ago I wrote a story about a secret society—you must remember it; but I never for a moment believed that there are such things. Anarchism, yes—Freemasonry—the Irish—'

'Those are mushrooms,' Smyth remarked, his lips giving out a trickle of thick cigar-smoke, languid as himself; while Crooks smoked a briar pipe.

'What! Freemasonry a mushroom?' — from Crooks — 'on the contrary—'

'Comparatively, of course, I meant. And I don't call those secret societies, of whose existence and objects everyone knows. Where's the secrecy? . . . But there are others.'

Crooks bent forward. He knew that Smyth was Cockney, as much a thing of London as was Charles Lamb, sometimes burrowing in some Slav night-club at the docks, or among 'Ye Merrie Men,' when supposed to be at holiday in Homburg: a being deeply initiated into London lore, knowing somewhat more behind those eyebrows of mild surprise than he ever mentioned at table: hence Crooks's interest; and his interest, like his other emotions, was usually shown.

'But in London?' he said. 'Really, now? Why have I never dropped across them? In Paris, yes—'

Smyth answered—his taciturnity sometimes melted when the subject was London—'Paris is to London as a shilling dictionary to the Encyclopaedia Britannica. Everything's in

London.'

'Except Paris'—from Crooks.

'Paris is, too: I could take you to the Bal Bullier within half a mile of here. Only, in Paris it has name and fame, in London it is lost.'

'But this "Rose" business—"secret societies"—you assure me they're a fact?'

'I am a member of two; I know of a third; and have suspicions of a fourth.' Smyth laughed a little to himself.

'That's three, say'—Crooks had animated eyes—'now, tell me how I can join them all!'

Smyth chuckled inwardly at this crude enthusiasm; and he said: 'You don't seem quite to realize—they are *secret* societies. There are more multi-millionaires—more experts in Becquerel rays—than members. To become a member of those I know is about as rare a thing as the conjunction of four planets; and requires long preparation. You can't go about "joining them" like that. One of them has consisted of sixteen members since the time of Edward II, another of twenty-three—'

'But what are they *for?*' Crooks fretfully cried. 'What's— what's their *motif,* their *idea?*'

'Different *motifs*. Most are benevolent, I think. All mystic.'

Then, why on earth are they secret, if they are benevolent?'

138

Crooks peered piercingly into it with the interest of the perplexed busybody: 'The mere fact that they are benevolent—'

'Different reasons for secrecy: some are secret to avoid—hanging sometimes.' Smyth showed his teeth in a silent laugh.

Then, I don't tumble,' from Crooks. 'Why need they avoid hanging, if they are benevolent?'

'Seems fairly obvious to me,' Smyth remarked, his straining lids half-shut behind his *pince-nez*: 'There are three types of really secret societies—absurd, obscene, and benevolent: and the benevolent ones can only be created for one reason—because Government, so far, is immature and defective. They assist Government by taking the law into their own hands, executing justice, doing good, in cases where Government can't, or won't, yet do it, and calling upon God to witness in a mystic mood.'

'Oho! Is that it? Then, they have my approval. And as to these "Friends of the Rose" tell me the particular—'

'It was a bad day for me,' Smyth interrupted, 'when I mentioned to you "Friends of the Rose," for you have left me no peace since. What business is it of yours? And what can you expect me to tell? Does the great Crooks take it for granted that secrets guarded six centuries will be blabbed to him for the asking? You may be perfectly certain, for instance, that "Friends of the Rose" is not really their name—though it is not unlike that. What can one tell? Perhaps I may tell you that the membership has always been limited to sixteen; or I may tell you that there is a certain apartment somewhere in London of whose existence only one man at a time— occasionally two—has known for five hundred years.

Crooks winked quick, hearing it; then threw his face about, frowning, fretted, almost offended, for he disliked being 'out of' anything. 'Apartment,' he muttered. . . . 'and who is that one man who knows?'

'The Primate of the Society.'

'Primate . . .' Crooks meditated it over the fire; then animatedly looked up to ask: 'Now, where can that apartment be?'

On which Smyth, tickled, let himself go into a sort of laugh, saying: 'What, want to take a lady there? I am sorry I can't tell you, if only because I have no notion myself. But when the Primate dies—he is a very old man—lives in Camden Town—I shall know.

'Oh, *you'll* be Primate then?'

Smyths lids lay closed. He made no answer.

'I should just like half-an-hour's interview with that "very old man who lives in Camden Town",' Crooks mentioned.

And Smyth answered: 'If you saw him hobbling along Gray's Inn Road, it would not occur to you to glance twice at him. London is like that. We brush shoulders with angels at Charing Cross, little divining the depths that some common-looking type has dived, the oddity of his destiny, his store of lore, his giftedness, or the dignity on his head. I know an old patternmaker in Wapping—'

But at this point Minna came in, and, as Crooks's attention was drawn off, Smyth suddenly stopped.

That was a Wednesday.

Now, on Fridays Smyth invariably left his office an hour earlier, dined at home, locked himself in his book-room for two hours, and then went out dumb, like a monk, not to come back till the morning hours.

Years had seen no break in this routine; but this Friday there was a break: for, for some unknown reason, Smyth was back at home before eleven.

In Victoria Street he glanced up at his windows on the second floor; noticed that the drawing-room light seemed low behind the blinds; and muttered something to himself.

He then went up by the lift, opened the flat-door with his key—and did it noiselessly, though he was *far* from admitting to himself that he did it noiselessly. He now glanced into the kitchen, and his eyebrows went higher because of the fact that it was in darkness. He passed, on padded carpet, to two other rooms — no one there: the servants had perhaps gone to the theatre. He then stepped down a passage to the drawing-room door, and, still without sound, turned the handle. But that door was locked: and his eyebrows went higher still.

Standing there, he seemed to come to a sudden decision: and walked sharply, softly, out of the flat.

Down below he stepped into a by-street where there is a Police Ambulance cot; and, standing in the shadow of this, looking toward Victoria Street, he waited.

After half-an-hour he saw Crooks come out of his 'Mansion'; slaw him walk away with quite an air of jauntiness; and presently saw his drawing-room lights turned on full.

He slept at the Hotel Victoria that night; and the next morning turned up at Covent House the same cold Smyth as ever—made a jest with the lift-man, going up to his office; and his sub-editor did not dream that day what was in him, nor that its name was Legion.

But in the afternoon his sister Minna, who had spent a day of wonderment and trembling, received a note 'by hand' from him:

'Dear Minna,

I regret that reasons have arisen which make it impossible for us to live any longer together. Pray write me by tomorrow whether you desire to stay on at the flat, or would rather that I took another for you.

Yours,
Crichton.'

So they parted.

She, knowing that he was attached to the flat, left it for one in Maida Vale, he settling an income upon her. From that night of the lowered lights he did not see her again—not for an instant. To her prayers for an explanation he made no answer.

But his pain proved more than he had bargained for, and he would have done better to have left those rooms which had known her presence. Though not very visible to others, there was a friendship and link between them extremely sacred and sweet; and he pretty soon discovered that, in sending her away, he had plucked out his right eye. Sometimes for days now he would absent himself from the office; his thin, palish face went pinched and paler; some grey began to mingle with his hair; his taciturnity turned to something like dumbness.

But he never relented; until, after six months, it came to his ears, through a doctor, that she was not well, and in a tragic fix. And then he wrote to her:

'Dear Minna,

I know everything: and whatever there is to forgive I

forgive. Please, dear, come back to my arms.

Yours,

Crichton.'

She would not at first; but then the wings of love proved stronger than her shrinkings: and she took herself back to the old flat.

But she was not well for she, too, had rued and gnashed, chewing the ashes of the fire of passion; so that daily he saw her vanishing like a shadow from him; and in a month she sighed at him, and died, leaving him a little girl to nurse.

As for Crooks, he was at Naples, and it was three months before he had definite knowledge that a child was born, a mother dead. Then he asserted himself. Since that Friday night of Smyths earlier return he had had no interview with Smyth, for Minna, as it were on her knees, had ever pleaded with him, 'Please, please, try not to meet Crichton!' But now Crooks asserted himself.

He sought out Smyth one night at the Savage, and, standing before Smyth's chair, said: 'Smyth, I must have the child.'

Smyth looked up from the slightly surprising thing in his *Standard* to the slightly surprising object before him, and said 'No.'

'Then, I have to see her sometimes—fair's fair.'

'If you like,' Smyth muttered. 'She is at my flat. Try not to see her often'—he read again.

So Crooks went and revolved philosophic thoughts over the insignificant stick of womanhood, that one could push into a jug: and she exclaimed on seeing his fat face, with hair stuck on it.

Then twice a month he went; and once, when, on meeting Smyth in Smyth's hall, he put out his hand, Smyth, with his eyebrows on high, let his long fingers be shaken. (Smyth, in fact, never participated in a hand-shake with any child of Adam, simply permitted and witnessed it, with surprise.)

And when this had happened several times in the course of a year, one night found Crooks seated by the fire, the child on his knee, over against Smyth, as of old. Without greatly caring, he had set himself to be friends again with Smyth, doing it in a patronizing mood, and so caring nothing for Smyth's surprise—nor, in truth, could he be sure that Smyth was more surprised than usual, since Smyth was for ever surprised. Moreover, Crooks's fame had lately swelled and mellowed; if he had an opinion on this or that matter, that was put into the newspapers; and he was puffed up, the fact being that the little men of his trade and grain have no essential self, nor impregnable self-estimation, which cannot be raised at all by any applause, nor depressed at all by any dispraise: but when the wind blows they are big, and when the wind lulls they are little. As for Crooks, at this time he felt that his presence honoured inventors and philosophers.

And 'Cluck, cluck,' he went, cantering his chick on his knee with a gee-up cackling; then 'I say, Smyth, did you ever become Primate of the Rose Society?'

'Yes,' Smyth replied with surprise.

'Ah, you did. So *you* have the secret now of that mysterious "Apartment"—'

'Yes,' Smyth replied with surprise.

'Then,' says Crooks to himself, 'I shall *set foot* in that apartment—sooner or later'; and he sat an hour with Smyth.

In this sort of relaxation they co-existed, until the midget Minna, fair and frail like its mother, could crawl, could walk, the months for mourning now long over, though Crichton Smyth still dressed in raiment of the raven—crape never more to leave that sleeve of his. Every Sunday sun-down found him in the Brompton Cemetery moping over a tomb; and most who saw him thought him cold; but some thought not. Meantime, Crooks dame fairly regularly to the flat; and he said one night by the fire: 'I shall leave off coming here, Smyth, if you don't talk to me. I have assumed that there can be no resentment left, since you realize that I loved Minna.'

Smyth's lips oozed smoke a minute; then: 'How many others did you love that year?'

'Several perhaps. I consider the question irrelevant—'

'How many have you loved since?'

'Several—many, perhaps. That is quite outside—'

'You are married.'

'Yes, but I am impatient of argument of the subject, Smyth. It simply means that your views on sex-relations are different from mine; and, as mine are the offspring of thought—'

'I am not "arguing",'—from Smyth with sleep-loaded lids: 'it is not a question of anyone's "views." I merely said that you are married, and it is a fact that, if a married man lets himself love a girl of the middle class, he runs a risk of killing her with shame. I do not say that it ought to be so—I am not arguing—I only state, what you know, that it *is* so—at present; and when a death occurs, you get murder. Of course, there is no law against it, but—' He stopped, passing his palm lazily across his raised forehead, his lids closed down, straining to open.

'Men are not exactly angels,' Crooks remarked.

'More like devils, some'—a mutter.

'Not referring to poor me?'

'Your existence seems to do a great deal of harm. I don't know that you do any good.'

'You don't know that my books do good?'

'No, I don't know. I know that men are already getting past "novels" without novelty, and that as soon as women cease to be children the last "novel" will be written. Yours are entertaining, I believe—'

'Not prophetic? Not vital?'

This tickled three of Smyth's ribs on the right side, and he let out on a breath of disdain: 'Lot of Simple-Simons we still are.'

But at this statement the little maid commenced to lament, and Crooks, handing her to her nurse, kissed her head, murmuring: 'I'll go.'

But, half-way to the door, he turned to say: 'What about that "Apartment" of yours, Smyth, that I am to be taken to? You said you'd consider it.'

Smyth's answer was a little singular. With a push of the lips, pettish, yet mixed with a smile, he said: 'Oh, you keep on about that!'

This was the *sixth* time that Crooks had asked—Smyth knew the number. At the first asking a flush of offence had touched Smyth's forehead at the cocky pushfulness that could prick Crooks to make such a request. But since then Smyth had begun to answer with a certain demur, a flirting reluctance, as of a girl who murmurs 'no,' but blushes 'yes.'

'*Oh, you keep on about that. . . .*'

'Where's the harm?' asked Crooks on his next visit. 'Provided you can absolutely rely upon my lifelong silence. My curiosity, of course, is intrinsically *literary*. Energize my imagination with an actual sight of the place, and I tell you what—I'll do a series of mystery-stories, and *The Westminster* shall have 'em.'

And Smyth, his lids closed but for a slit that rested on Crooks, answered: 'Ah, Crooks, don't tempt me.'

It was, then, a question of temptation now? Crooks felt exultation. Had not the sister yielded to his tempting? The brother should be his conquest, too. . . .

But on the next occasion of Smyth's temptation, Smyth said with a laugh: 'You don't apparently care whether you urge me to the breach of a vow of office! And you do it with that same facile callousness with which you break your own marriage-vow.'

'Smyth, you will not do as a conscience—you are too pale,' said Crooks. 'Please leave our evil marriage-customs out of the discussion. As to your "vow of office," did you not yourself tell me that sometimes *two* men have known the alleged "Apartment"?'

'Well, yes, I think I did say so. And you conceive, do you, that *you* have a right to be one of the two? Well, perhaps you have—I'll look into the question. But, if ever I do take you, I hope you are not nervous.'

'Fancy a nervous E. P. Crooks! What is there to see, then?'

'It is a little—lethal.'

'Then, I'm the man. But when?'

'I haven't said yes. Give one time. I have to get the approval of others. . . .'

But only three weeks afterwards Smyth yielded. 'Very well,' he said: you shall see it; the thing's settled; your imagination shall be "energized," as you call it. But you are not permitted to know *where* the room is: you have to go to it blindfold. And, by the way, you must go disguised: just hang a beard round your ears—that'll do. And be before the Temple Church on Tuesday night, to hear the Law Courts clock strike eleven.'

'*Fiet!*' Crooks cried.

That Tuesday night in October a high wind blew, and by the light of a moon that flew to encounter flying troops of cloud, Crooks stood looking at those eight old tombs, and the circular west-end of the church. The Strand river had thinned now to a trickle of feet: in there in the secrecy of the Inn not a step passed; and Crooks felt upon him the mood of adventure: London was partly Baghdad; this an Arabian night: some time or other he'd make 'copy' of the mood of it. To be disguised, too, was quite novel to nim: anon he pawed his false beard with a mock pomposity; then he had the thought: 'But why, after all, the disguise?'; and just then eleven struck.

At its last stroke a step was on the paving, and Crichton

Smyth with his crape and raven dress was there. He put finger to lip when Crooks began to say something, beckoned, and Crooks followed out through Hare Court, by Middle Temple Lane, past the under-porter's lodge; when Smyth got into a coupé brougham waiting by the Griffin, Crooks followed in.

'I must blindfold you here,' Smyth said at his ear.

'There remains the inward eye,'—from Crooks—'blindfold away.'

At once Smyth produced two pads of black cotton, and a black ribbon that had two narrower ribbons sewed to its ends; cottons and ribbon he tied over Crooks's eyes and nose: and now it could be seen that the broad ribbon had crimson borders, and three roses embroidered on it.

As soon as it was secured, Smyth, unknown to Crooks, slipped a strip of brass-plate inside the band of Crooks's bowler-hat—a brass-plate on which were etched the words: 'Edgar Crichton Smyth, P.' Whereupon the driver, as if he had waited for all this, went forward without being ordered.

But Crooks understood that they were going eastward. He heard Bennett's Clock quite near above strike the quarter-past. And presently the following words were uttered within that brougham

Crooks: Talk to me. I am lost in darkness. Silence must be awful to the blind.

Smyth: I don't want to talk. This is not a night like every night for you and me.

Crooks: You think something of that 'Apartment' of yours!

Smyth: It is not an Apartment with 'To Let' in the window. It has no window. I hope you have said your prayers.

Crooks: Men of my birth have no need to say prayers, Smyth. Behind and underneath we are essentially religious; and our existence, properly understood, is a prayer.

Smyth: Good thing you are religious behind.

Crooks: Did you not *know* that I am?

Smyth: No, how was I to know? You aren't where one sees you.

Crooks: Smyth, you are the most—

Smyth: Don't chatter.

Here Crooks could hear a tram droning somewhere through the humdrum plod-clap, plod-clap, of the brougham-horse's hoofs on asphalt; he thought to himself: 'We must be somewhere in Whitechapel; and presently they spoke again:

Crooks: Is it far now?

Smyth: Ten minutes.

Crooks: I don't like the blindfolding, though—and, by the way, what is the disguise for? I understand the blindfold, but why the disguise?

Smyth: You will soon guess why.

Crooks: Your disguise is a mystery, and your blindfolding a plague. Ah, it must be sad to be blind!

Smyth: What about being dead?

Crooks: The dead don't know that they are blind, but the blind know that they are dead. Oh, it is a great thing to see the sun! to be alive, and see it. People don't realize, because the universe is not meant for men to see, but for the lords of older orbs than this to cast down their crowns before. Tomorrow morning when I have back my sight, I shall build me an altar.

Smyth: Don't make any vows at it.

Crooks: Certainly, Smyth, you are the most surly and cynical—

Smyth: We get out here.

On this the brougham, without order, stopped; Smyth, having got out, led out Crooks; and, without order, the brougham rolled away.

As it had made several turnings, Crooks did not know in what district of London he now was—he knew that it was East. But no sound of foot-falls passing here; only, he could hear a rush of machinery going on somewhere.

'Those are alternators driven by steam-turbines,' he said. 'But are we in a street?'

'Sh-h, don't talk.' said Smyth.

Crooks next felt himself led by the hand over what seemed

to be cobble-stones, where the feet echoed, and there was a draught, so that he thought he must be under some tunnel, or vault. Then he felt himself in the open again, still going over old cobble-stones; and still the thump and rush of machinery reached the ear from somewhere. As for Smyth, he uttered not a word, and would listen to none.

Then there was a stoppage: Crooks knew that a door was being unlocked. And, hearing now a click at his ear, he could guess that Smyth had switched on the light of a torch.

He was next led over bare boards in some place that had a smell of soap and candles, tar and benzoline; and twice his steps tripped over what seemed to be empty bags. Then he was led slowly down some board steps; at the bottom of which Smyth stooped to unlock something—apparently a trapdoor in the ground.

Through this Crooks was led down, Smyth now saying to him: 'Hold my jacket; these steps are narrow'—and Crooks went down some steep steps of stone, each step a jolt, where he ceased to hear the beat of the machinery.

After this he passed through a passage, apparently of hardened marl, markedly damp and clammy, and uneven to the feet, where even sightless eyes could see and feel the thickness of the darkness; at the far end of which Smyth was again known to open some door—evidently a very heavy one—whose lock gnashed at the key, whose hinges chattered.

From which point Crooks was led up steps so narrow, that he could easily feel the wall on either hand, they going now in single file.

To these steps there seemed no end—up and still up; and soon Crooks was afresh conscious of the throb and thresh of steam-machinery, jumbled with the hum of generators making their jew's-harp music: this business and to-do seeming to increase on the ear, and then, as still up they climbed, seeming to die away. Whenever they came to a landing or passage, Crooks, who was fat, and panted, said to himself 'at last'; but several times he had to recommence the climb; and he thought to himself 'Can it be the Tower of London? We are in some tower, within the thickness of the wall'; but he did not say anything: a mood of utter dumbness had come upon him.

At last, in moving along a passage over stone floor, he being then in front of Smyth, he stumbled, apparently in dust or rubbish; the next moment he was stopped, butting upon wall; and 'Hallo,' said he, 'what's this?'

There was no reply. . . .

Waiting against the wall for guidance, Crooks was conscious of a clang behind him, as of a massive portal slammed, and of the croak of a rusty lock being coaxed by a key. Then he was aware of a scraping, as if a ponderous object was being dragged across the corridor; and simultaneously

155

-he was aware of an odour under his nose.

'Smyth!' he called out: 'are you there?'

There was no reply. . . .

Now he was aware of a match being struck, then of another, and another. By this time his bones were as cold as the stones that enclosed him.

He suddenly cried out 'Smyth! I am going to take the bandage off!'

Still there was no answer but some moments afterwards there burst upon his startled heart a most bizarre noise, a babbling, or lalling, half-talk, half-song, in some unknown tongue—from Smyth. The next instant Crooks had the bandage snatched from his eyes.

There was light—a pink light—brilliant at first to him; and by it he instantly realized that he was interned. He stood in a room of untooled ashlar some fourteen feet square, with a doorway three feet wide looking down a corridor three feet wide. It was the door of this doorway that had been slammed; but he could still look out, since the door had a hole in its iron—a hole Gothic in shape like the door itself; and outside the door stood an old pricket-candlestick of iron supporting seven candles, all alight, higher than a man's head, occupying all the breadth of the corridor.

Crooks understood that that scraping sound he had heard must have been due to the placing of the candlestick in position, and that the striking of the matches had been for lighting the seven candles, each of which had, before and behind it, a screen of pink porcelain with a pattern of roses—two perpendicular rows of roses—so that, as the candles got lower, they would still glow through a rose.

All this he noticed in some moments; also that there was a handbag open on the floor, out of which he assumed that Smyth had got the sort of linen amice, dotted with roses, which he now wore round his shoulders; moreover, in some moments it had entered his consciousness that the dust and rubbish into which he had stumbled was made of the bones and dust and clothes of men who had ended their days there; moreover, he noticed that, hanging before the hole in the portal, was an old Toledo *puñal* of damascened steel, and he understood that this was mercifully meant for his use against himself, if he so chose. If he had doubted this—if he had cherished a hope—it would have vanished when he saw what was hanging on the shaft of the candlestick—a bit of ebony, or black marble, on which had been scribbled in red pencil:

MINNA AND FOUR OTHERS

But what most froze the current of Crooks's blood was the horrid comedy of Smyth's psalmodying and dancing in his amice a yard beyond the candles, like one putting forth a spell of 'woven paces and of waving hands,' his head cast back, his gaze on Heaven—his pince-nez on his nose! But in what occult Chaldæ;an was that bleating to Moloch and Baal that his tongue baa'd and bleated? Crooks knew some languages but this recitative had no affinity with any speech of men which he had ever conceived; and then that antic fandango-tangle of writhing palms and twining thighs that went on with the psalming, like some entranced wight steadily treading the treadmill of dance in the land of the tarantula—a piece of witchcraft as antique and aboriginal as torch-lit orgies of Sheba and Egypt . . .

His throat straining out of the hole—his eyes straining out of his head—Crooks sent out to that dread dancer the whisper: '*Smyth, don't do it, Smyth . . .*'

He might as well have whispered to the dust and ashes in which he stood.

After three minutes the ritual ceased; Smyth stood another minute, his brow bowed down, with muttering mouth; then took off and put the amice into a handbag; picked up and put on his hat; and, without speaking, went away, leaving the candles watching there, as for a wake.

THE WIZARD

'The following account of a rural American spell from which his wife was rescued was given to me by a New England resident:

"The wizard," to quote the exact words of my informant, "threw a stick on a chest; the stick bounded like a trapball three times; then he opened the chest, took out something looking like dust or clay, and put it into a cup with water over a fire; then he poured it over a board (after chopping it three times), which he then put up beneath the shingles of the house. Returning to the chest he took a piece of old chain, near the length of my hand, took a hoe and buried the chain near the sill of the door of my wife's house where she would pass; then he went away. I saw my wife coming and called to her not to pass, and to go for a hoe and dig up the place. She did this, and I took up the chain, which burned the ends of all my fingers clean off. The same night the conjuror came back: my wife took two half dollars and a quarter in silver and threw them on the ground before him. The man seemed as if he was shocked, and then offered her his hand, which she refused to take, as I had bid her not to let him touch her. He left and never came to the house again. The spell was broken." '

M. DANIEL CONWAY,
Demonology and Devil Lore

WITCHES' HOLLOW

H. P. LOVECRAFT

District School Number Seven stood on the very edge of that wild country which lies west of Arkham. It stood in a little grove of trees, chiefly oaks and elms with one or two maples; in one direction the road led to Arkham, in the other it dwindled away into the wild, wooded country which always looms darkly on that western horizon. It presented a warmly attractive appearance to me when first I saw it on my arrival as the new teacher early in September, 1920, though it had no distinguishing architectural feature and was in every respect the replica of thousands of country schools scattered throughout New England, a compact, conservative building painted white, so that it shone forth from among the trees in the midst of which it stood.

It was an old building at that time, and no doubt has since been abandoned or torn down. The school district has now been consolidated, but at that time it supported this school in somewhat niggardly a manner, skimping and saving on every necessity. Its standard readers, when I came there to teach, were still *McGuffey's Eclectic Readers*, in editions published before the turn of the century. My charges added up to twenty-seven. There were Allens and Whateleys and Perkinses, Dunlocks and Abbotts and Talbots—and there was Andrew Potter.

I cannot now recall the precise circumstances of my especial notice of Andrew Potter. He was a large boy for his age, very dark of mien, with haunting eyes and a shock of touselled black hair. His eyes brooded upon me with a kind of different quality which at first challenged me but ultimately left me strangely uneasy. He was in the fifth grade, and it did not take me long to discover that he could very easily advance into the seventh or eighth, but made no effort to do so. He seemed to have only a casual tolerance for his schoolmates, and for their part, they respected him, but not out of affection so much as what struck me soon as fear. Very soon thereafter, I began to understand that this strange lad held for me the same kind of amused tolerance that he held for his schoolmates.

Perhaps it was inevitable that the challenge of this pupil should lead me to watch him as surreptitiously as I could, and as the circumstances of teaching a one-room school permitted. As a result, I became aware of a vaguely disquieting fact; from time to time, Andrew Potter responded to some stimulus beyond the apprehension of my senses, reacting precisely as if someone had called to him, sitting up, growing alert, and wearing the air of someone listening to sounds beyond my own hearing, in the same attitude assumed by animals hearing sounds beyond the pitch-levels of the human ear.

My curiosity quickened by this time, I took the first opportunity to ask about him. One of the eighth-grade boys, Wilbur Dunlock, was in the habit on occasion of staying after school and helping with the cursory cleaning that the room needed.

'Wilbur,' I said to him late one afternoon. 'I notice you don't seem to pay much attention to Andrew Potter, none of you. Why?'

He looked at me, a lttle distrustfully, and pondered his answer before he shrugged and replied, 'He's not like us.'

'In what way?'

He shook his head. 'He don't care if we let him play with us or not. He don't want to.'

He seemed reluctant to talk, but by dint of repeated questions I drew from him certain spare information. The Potters lived deep in the hills to the west along an all but abandoned branch of the main road that led through the hills. Their farm stood in a little valley locally known as Witches' Hollow which Wilbur described as 'a bad place.' There were only four of them — Andrew, an older sister, and their parents. They did not 'mix' with other people of the district, not even with the Dunlocks, who were their nearest neighbours, living but half a mile from the school itself, and thus, perhaps, four miles from Witches' Hollow, with woods separating the two farms.

More than this he could not—or would not—say.

About a week later, I asked Andrew Potter to remain after school. He offered no objection, appearing to take my request as a matter of course. As soon as the other children had gone, he came up to my desk and stood there waiting, his dark eyes fixed expectantly on me, and just the shadow of a smile on his full lips.

'I've been studying your grades, Andrew,' I said, 'and it seems to me that with only á little effort you could skip into the sixth—perhaps even the seventh—grade. Wouldn't you like to make that effort?'

He shrugged.

'What do you intend to do when you get out of school?'

He shrugged again.

'Are you going to high school in Arkham?'

He considered me with eyes that seemed suddenly piercing in their keenness, all lethargy gone. 'Mr Williams, I'm here because there's a law says I have to be,' he answered. 'There's no law says I have to go to high school.'

'But aren't you interested?' I pressed him.

'What I'm interested in doesn't matter. It's what my folks want that counts.'

'Well, I'm going to talk to them.' I decided on the moment. 'Come along. I'll take you home.'

For a moment something like alarm sprang into his expression, but in seconds it diminished and gave way to that air of watchful lethargy so typical of him. He shrugged and stood waiting while I slipped my books and papers into the schoolbag I habitually carried. Then he walked docilely to the car with me and got in, looking at me with a smile that could only be described as superior.

We rode through the woods in silence, which suited the mood that came upon me as soon as we had entered the hills, for the trees pressed close upon the road, and the deeper we went, the darker grew the wood, perhaps as much because of the lateness of that October day as because of the thickening of the trees. From relatively open glades, we plunged into an ancient wood, and when at last we turned down the side road—little more than a lane—to which Andrew silently pointed, I found that I was driving through a growth of very old and strangely deformed trees. I had to proceed with caution; the road was so little used that underbrush crowded upon it from both sides, and, oddly, I recognized little of it, for all my studies in botany, though once I thought I saw saxifrage, curiously mutated. I drove abruptly, without warning, into the yard before the Potter house.

The sun was now lost behind the wall of trees, and the house stood on a kind of twilight. Beyond it stretched a few fields, strung out up the valley; in one, there were cornshocks, in another stubble, in yet another pumpkins. The house itself was forbidding, low to the ground, with half a second storey, gambrel-roofed, with shuttered windows, and the outbuildings stood gaunt and stark, looking as if they had never been used. The entire farm looked deserted; the only sign of life was in a few chickens that scratched at the earth behind the house.

Had it not been that the lane along which we had travelled ended here, I would have doubted that we had reached the Potter house. Andrew flashed a glance at me, as if he sought some expression on my face to convey to him what I thought. Then he jumped lightly from the car, leaving me to follow.

He went into the house ahead of me. I heard him announce me.

'Brought the teacher. Mr. Williams.'

There was no answer.

Then abruptly I was in the room, ht only by an old-fashioned kerosene lamp, and there were the other three Potters—the father, a tall, stoop-shouldered man, grizzled and greying, who could not have been more than forty but looked much, much older, not so much physically as

psychically—the mother, an almost obscenely fat woman—
and the girl, slender, tall, and with that same air of watchful
waiting that I had noticed in Andrew.

Andrew made the brief introductions, and the four of
them stood or sat, waiting upon what I had to say, and
somewhat uncomfortably suggesting in their attitudes that I
say it and get out.

'I wanted to talk to you about Andrew,' I said. 'He shows
great promise, and he could be moved up a grade or two if
he'd study a little more.'

My words were not welcomed.

'I believe he's smart enough for eighth grade,' I went on,
and stopped.

'If he 'uz in eighth grade,' said his father, 'he's be havin' to
go to high school 'fore he uz old enough to git outa goin' to
school. That's the law. They told me.'

I could not help thinking of what Wilbur Dunlock had
told me of the reclusiveness of the Potters, and as I listened
to the elder Potter, and thought of what I had heard, I was
suddenly aware of a kind of tension among them, and a
subtle alteration in their attitude. The moment the father
stopped talking, there was a singular harmony of attitude—
all four of them seemed to be listening to some inner voice,
and I doubt that they heard my protest at all.

'You can't expect a boy as smart as Andrew just to come

back here,' I said.

'Here's good enough,' said old Potter. 'Besides, he's ours. And don't ye go talkin' 'bout us now, Mr. Williams.'

He spoke with so latently menacing an undercurrent in his voice that I was taken aback. At the same time I was increasingly aware of a miasma of hostility, not proceeding so much from any one or all four of them, as from the house and its setting themselves.

'Thank you,' I said. 'I'll be going.'

I turned and went out, Andrew at my heels.

Outside, Andrew said softly, 'You shouldn't be talking about us, Mr. Williams. Pa gets mad when he finds out. You talked to Wilbur Dunlock.'

I was arrested at getting into the car. With one foot on the running board, I turned. 'Did he say so?' I asked.

He shook his head. 'You did, Mr. Williams,' he said, and backed away. 'It's not what he thinks, but what he might do.'

Before I could speak again, he had darted into the house.

For a moment I stood undecided. But my decision was made for me. Suddenly, in the twilight, the house seemed to burgeon with menace, and all the surrounding woods seemed to stand waiting but to bend upon me. Indeed, I was aware of a rustling, like the whispering of wind, in all the wood, though no wind stirred, and from the house itself came a malevolence like the blow of a fist. I got into the car and drove away, with that impression of malignance at my back like the hot breath of a ravaging pursuer.

I reached my room in Arkham at last, badly shaken. Seen in retrospect, I had undergone an unsettling psychic experience; there was no other explanation for it. I had the unavoidable conviction that, however blindly, I had thrust myself in far deeper waters than I knew, and the very unexpectedness of the experience made it the more chilling. I could not eat for the wonder of what went on in that house in Witches' Hollow, of what it was that bound the family together, chaining them to that place, preventing a promising lad like Andrew Potter even from the most fleeting wish to leave that dark valley and go out into a brighter world.

I lay for most of that night, sleepless, filled with a nameless dread for which all explanation eluded me, and when I slept at last my sleep was filled with hideously disturbing dreams, in which beings far beyond my mundane imagination held the stage, and cataclysmic events of tne utmost terror and horror took place. And when I rose next morning, I felt that somehow I had touched upon a world totally alien to my kind.

I reached the school early that morning, But Wilbur Dunlock was there before me. His eyes met mine with sad reproach. I could not imagine what had happened to disturb this usually friendly pupil.

'You shouldn't a told Andrew Potter we talked about him,' he said with a kind of unhappy resignation.

'I didn't, Wilbur.'

'I know I didn't. So you must have,' he said. And then, 'Six of our cows got killed last night, and the shed where they were was crushed down on 'em.'

I was momentarily too startled to reply. 'A sudden windstorm,' I began, but he cut me off.

'Weren't no wind last night, Mr. Williams. And the cows were *smashed.*'

'You surely cannot think that the Potters had anything to do with this, Wilbur,' I cried.

He gave me a weary look—the look of one who *knows*, meeting the glance of one who should know but cannot understand, and said nothing more.

This was even more upsetting than my experience of the previous evening. He at least was convinced that there was a connection between our conversation about the Potter family and the Dunlocks' loss of half a dozen cows. And he was convinced with so deep a conviction that I knew without trying that nothing I could say would shake it.

When Andrew Potter came in, I looked in vain for any sign that anything out of the ordinary had taken place since last I had seen him.

Somehow I got through that day. Immediately after the close of the school session, I hastened into Arkham and went to the office of the *Arkham Gazette*, the editor of which had been kind enough, as a member of the local District Board of Education, to find my room for me. He was an elderly man, almost seventy, and might presumably know what I wanted to find out.

My appearance must have conveyed something of my agitation, for when I walked into his office, his eyebrows lifted, and he said, 'What's got your dander up, Mr. Williams?'

I made some attempt to dissemble, since I could put my hand upon nothing tangible, and, viewed in the cold light of day, what I might have said would have sounded almost hysterical to an impartial listener. I said only, 'I'd like to know something about a Potter family that lives in Witches' Hollow, west of the school.'

He gave me an enigmatic glance. 'Never heard of old Wizard Potter?' he asked. And, before I could answer, he went on, 'No, of course, you're from Brattleboro. We could hardly expect Vermonters to know about what goes on in the Massachusetts back country. He lived there first. An old man when I first knew him. And these Potters were distant relatives, lived in Upper Michigan, inherited the property and came to live there when Wizard Potter died.'

'But what do you know about them?' I persisted.

'Nothing but what everybody else knows,' he said. 'When they came, they were nice friendly people. Now they talk to nobody, seldom come out—and there's all that talk about missing animals from the farms in the district. The people tie that all up.'

Thus begun, I questioned him at length.

I listened to a bewildering enigma of half-told tales, hints, legends and lore utterly beyond my comprehension. What seemed to be incontrovertible was a distant cousinship between Wizard Potter and one Wizard Whateley of nearby Dunwich—'a bad lot,' the editor called him; the solitary way of life of old Wizard Potter, and the incredible length of time he had lived; the fact that people generally shunned Witches' Hollow. What seemed to be sheer fantasy was the superstitious lore—that Wizard Potter had 'called something down from the sky, and it lived with him or in him until he died';—that a late traveller, found in a dying state along the main road, had gasped out something about 'that thing with the feelers—slimy, rubbery thing with the suckers on its feelers' that came out of the woods and attacked him—and a good deal more of the same kind of lore.

When he finished, the editor scribbled a note to the librarian at Miskatonic University in Arkham, and handed it to me. 'Tell him to let you look at that book. You may learn something.' He shrugged. 'And you may not. Young people now-days take the world with a lot of salt.'

I went supperless to pursue my search for the special knowledge I felt I needed, if I were to save Andrew Potter for a better life. For it was this rather than the satisfaction of my curiosity that impelled me! I made my way to the library of Miskatonic University, looked up the librarian, and handed him the editor's note.

The old man gave me a sharp look, said, 'Wait here, Mr. Williams,' and went off with a ring of keys. So the book, whatever it was, was kept under lock and key.

I waited for what seemed an interminable time. I was now beginning to feel some hunger, and to question my unseemly haste—and yet I felt that there was little time to be lost, though I could not define the catastrophe I hoped to avert. Finally the librarian came, bearing an ancient tome, and brought it around to a table within his range of vision. The book's title was in Latin—*Necronomicon*—though its author was evidently an Arabian, *Abdul Alhazred*, and its text was in somewhat archaic English.

I began to read with interest which soon turned to complete bewilderment. The book evidently concerned ancient, alien races, invaders of earth, great mythical beings called Ancient Ones and Elder Gods, with outlandish names like Cthulhu and Hastur, Shub-Niggurath and Azathoth, Dagon and

Ithaqua and Wendigo and Cthugha, all involved in some kind of plan to dominate earth and served by some of its peoples—the Tcho-Tcho, and the Deep Ones, and the like. It was a book filled with cabbalistic lore, incantations, and what purported to be an account of a great interplanetary battle between the Elder Gods and the Ancient Ones and of the survival of cults and servitors in isolated and remote places on our planet as well as on sister planets. What this rigmarole had to do with my immediate problem, with the ingrown and strange Potter family and their longing for solitude and their anti-social way of life, was completely beyond me.

How long I would have gone on reading, I do not know. I was interrupted presently by the awareness of being studied by a stranger, who stood not far from me with his eyes moving from the book I was busy reading to me. Having caught my eye, he made so bold as to come over to my side.

'Forgive me,' he said, 'But what in this book interests a country school teacher?'

'I wonder now myself,' I said.

He introduced himself as Professor Martin Keane. 'I may say, sir,' he added, 'that I know this book practically by heart.'

'A farrago of superstitution.'

'Do you think so?'

173

'Emphatically.'

'You have lost the quality of wonder, Mr. Williams. Tell me, if you will, what brought you to this book—'

I hesitated, but Professor Keane's personality was persuasive and inspired confidence.

'Let us walk, if you don't mind,' I said.

He nodded.

I returned the book to the librarian, and joined my new-found friend. Haltingly, as clearly as I could, I told him about Andrew Potter, the house in Witches' Hollow, my strange psychic experience—even the curious coincidence of Dunlock's cows. To all this he listened without interruption, indeed, with a singular absorption. I explained at last that my motive in looking into the background of Witches' Hollow was solely to do something for my pupil.

'A little research,' he said, 'would have informed you that many strange events have taken place in such remote places as Dunwich and Innsmouth—even Arkham and Witches' Hollow,' he said when I finished. 'Look around you at these ancient houses with their shuttered rooms and ill-lit fanlights. How many strange events have taken place under those gambrel roofs! We snail never know. But let us put aside the question of belief! One may not need to see the embodiment of evil to believe in it, Mr. Williams. I should like to be of some small service to the boy in this matter.

May I?'

'By all means!'

'It may be perilous—to you as well as to him.'

'I am not concerned about myself.'

'But I assure you, it cannot be any more perilous to the boy than his present position. Even death for him is less perilous.'

'You speak in riddles, Professor.'

'Let it be better so, Mr. Williams. But come—we are at my residence. Pray come in.'

We went into one of those ancient houses of which Professor Keane had spoken. I walked into the musty past, for the rooms were filled with books and all manner of antiquities. My host took me into what was evidently his sitting-room, swept a chair clear of books, and invited me to wait while he busied himself on the second floor.

He was not, however, gone very long—not even long enough for me to assimilate the curious atmosphere of the room in which I waited. When he came back he carried what I saw at once were objects of stone, roughly in the shape of five-pointed stars. He put five of them into my hands.

'Tomorrow after school—if the Potter boy is there—you must contrive to touch him with one of these, and keep it fixed upon him,' said my host. There are two other conditions. You must keep one of these at least on your person at all times, and you must keep all thought of the stone and what you are about to do out of your mind. These beings have a telepathic sense—an ability to read your thoughts.'

Startled, I recalled Andrew's charging me with having talked about them with Wilbur Dunlock.

'Should I not know what these are?' I asked.

'If you can abate your doubts for the time being,' my host answered with a grim smile. These stones are among the thousands bearing the Seal of R'lyeh which closed the prisons of the Ancient Ones. They are the seals of the Elder Gods.'

'Professor Keane, the age of superstition is past,' I protested.

'Mr. Williams—the wonder of life and its mysteries is never past,' he retorted. 'If the stone has no meaning, it has no power. If it has no power, it cannot affect young Potter. And it cannot protect you.'

'From what?'

'From the power behind the malignance you felt at the house in Witches' Hollow,' he answered. 'Or was this too superstition?' He smiled. 'You need not answer. I know your answer. If something happens when you put the stone upon the boy, he cannot be allowed to go back home. You must bring him here to me. Are you agreed?'

'Agreed,' I answered.

That next day was interminable, not only because of the imminence of crisis, but because it was extremely difficult to keep my mind blank before the inquiring gaze of Andrew Potter. Moreover, I was conscious as never before of the wall of pulsing malignance at my back, emanating from the wild country there, a tangible menace hidden in a pocket of the dark hills. But the hours passed, however slowly, and just before dismissal I asked Andrew Potter to wait after the others had gone.

And again he assented with that casual air tantamount almost to insolence, so that I was compelled to ask myself whether he were worth 'saving' as I thought of saving him in the depths of my mind.

But I persevered. I had hidden the stone in my car, and, once the others were gone, I asked Andrew to step outside with me.

At this point I felt both helpless and absurd. I, a college graduate, about to attempt what for me seemed inevitably the kind of mumbo-jumbo that belonged to the African wilderness. And for a few moments, as I walked stiffly from the school house toward the car I almost flagged, almost simply invited Andrew to get into the car to be driven home.

But I did not. I reached the car with Andrew at my heels, reached in, seized a stone to slip into my own pocket, seized another, and turned with lightning rapidity to press the stone to Andrew's forehead.

Whatever I expected to happen, it was not what took place.

For, at the touch of the stone, an expression of the utmost horror shone in Andrew Potter's eyes; in a trice, his gave way to poignant anguish; a great cry of terror burst from his lips. He flung his arms wide, scattering his books, wheeled as far as he could with my hold upon him, shuddered, and would have fallen, had I not caught him and lowered him, foaming at the mouth, to the ground. And then I was conscious of a great, cold wind which whirled about us and was gone, bending the grasses and the flowers, rippling the edge of the wood, and tearing away the leaves at the outer band of trees.

Driven by my own terror, I lifted Andrew Potter into the car, laid the stone on his chest, and drove as fast as I could into Arkham, seven miles away. Professor Keane was waiting, no whit surprised at my coming. And he had expected that I would bring Andrew Potter, for he had made a bed ready for him, and together we put him into it, after which Keane administered a sedative.

Then he turned to me. 'Now then, there's no time to be lost. They'll come to look for him—the girl probably first. We must get back to the school house at once.'

But now the full meaning and horror of what had happened to Andrew Potter had dawned upon me, and I was so shaken that it was necessary for Keane to push me from the room and half drag me out of the house. And again, as I set down these words so long after the terrible events of that night, I find myself trembling with that apprehension and fear which seize hold of a man who comes for the first time face to face with the vast unknown and knows how puny and meaningless he is against that cosmic immensity. I knew in that moment that what I had read in that forbidden book at the Miskatonic Library was not a farrago of superstition, but the key to a hitherto unsuspected revelation perhaps far, far older than mankind in the universe. I did not dare to think of what Wizard Potter had called down from the sky.

I hardly heard Professor Keane's words as he urged me to discard my emotional reaction and think of what had happened in scientific, more clinical fashion. After all, I had now accomplished my objective—Andrew Potter was saved. But to insure it, he must be made free of the others, who would surely follow him and find him. I thought only of what waiting horror that quartet of country people from Michigan had walked into when they came to take up possession of the solitary farm in Witches' Hollow.

I drove blindly back to the school. There, at Professor Keane's behest, I put on the lights and sat with the door open to the warm night, while he concealed himself behind the building to wait upon their coming. I had to steel myself in order to blank out my mind and take up that vigil.

On the edge of night, the girl came . . .

And after she had undergone the same experience as her brother, and lay beside the desk, the star-shaped stone on her breast, their father showed up in the doorway. All was darkness now, and he carried a gun. He had no need to ask what had happened; he *knew*. He stood wordless, pointed to his daughter and the stone on her breast, and raised his gun. His inference was plain—if I did not remove the stone, he meant to shoot. Evidently this was the contingency the professor expected, for he came upon Potter from the rear and touched him with the stone.

Afterwards we waited for two hours—in vain, for Mrs. Potter.

'She isn't coming,' said Professor Keane at last. 'She harbours the seat of its intelligence—I had thought it would be the man. Very well—we have no choice—we must go to Witches' Hollow. These two can be left here.'

We drove through the darkness, making no attempt at secrecy, for the professor said the 'thing' in the house in the Hollow 'knew' we were coming but could not reach us past the talisman of the stone. We went through that close pressing forest, down the narrow lane where the queer undergrowth seemed to reach out toward us in the glow of the head lights, into the Potter yard.

The house stood dark save for a wan glow of lamplight in one room.

Professor Keane leaped from the car with his little bag of star-shaped stones, and went around sealing the house—with a stone at each of the two doors, and one at each of the windows, through one of which we could see the woman sitting at the kitchen table—stolid, watchful, *aware*, no longer dissembling, looking unlike that tittering woman I had seen in this house not long ago, but rather like some great sentient beast at bay.

When he had finished, my companion went around to the front and, by means of brush collected from the yard and piled against the door, set fire to the house heedless of my protests.

Then he went back to the window to watch the woman, explaining that only fire could destroy the elemental force, but that he hoped, still, to save Mrs. Potter. 'Perhaps you'd better not watch, Williams.'

I did not heed him. Would that I had—and so spared myself the dreams that invade my sleep even yet! I stood at the window behind him and watched what went on in that room—for the smell of smoke was now permeating the house. Mrs. Potter—or what animated her gross body—

started up, went awkwardly to the back door, retreated, to the window, retreated from it, and came back to the centre of the room, between the table and the wood stove, not yet fired against the coming cold. There she fell to the floor, heaving and writhing.

The room filled slowly with smoke, hazing about the yellow lamp, making the room indistinct—but not indistinct enough to conceal completely what went on in the course of that terrible struggle on the floor, where Mrs. Potter threshed about as if in mortal convulsion and slowly, half visibly, something or other took shape—an incredible amorphous mass, only half glimpsed in the smoke, tentacled, shimmering, with a cold intelligence and a physical coldness that I could feel through the window. The thing rose like a cloud above the now motionless body of Mrs. Potter, and then fell upon the stove and drained into it like vapour!

'The stove!' cried Professor Keane, and fell back.

Above us, out of the chimney, came a spreading blackness, like smoke, gathering itself briefly there. Then it hurtled like a lightning bolt aloft, into the stars, in the direction of the Hyades, back to. mat place from which old Wizard Potter had called it into himself, away from where it had lain in wait for the Potters to come from Upper Michigan and afford it new host on the face of earth.

We managed to get Mrs. Potter out of the house, much

shrunken now, but alive.

On the remainder of that night's events there is no need to to dwell—how the professor waited until fire had consumed the house to collect his store of star-shaped stones, of the reuniting of the Potter family—freed from the curse of Witches' Hollow and determined never to return to that haunted valley—of Andrew, who, when we came to waken him, was talking in his sleep of 'great winds that fought and tore' and a 'place by the Lake of Hali where they live in glory forever.'

What it was that old Wizard Potter had called down from the stars, I lacked the courage to ask, but I knew that it touched upon secrets better left unknown to the races of men, secrets I would never have become aware of had I not chanced to take District School Number Seven, and had among my pupils the strange boy who was Andrew Potter.

A LOVE INVOCATION

'*A woman who wishes to gain the love of a man should procure the following materials from neighbours with whom she has never eaten: coriander, carraway, gum of terebinth, lime, cummin, verdigris, myrrh, some blood of an animal whose throat has been cut, and a piece of broom from a cemetery. On a dark night she is to go into the country with a lighted brazier and throw these different articles one after another into the fire, speaking these words: "O coriander, bring him mad! O carraway bring him wandering without success! O mastic, raise in his heart anguish and tears! O white lime, make his heart wakeful in disquietude! O cummin, bring him possessed! O verdigris, kindle the fire of his heart! O myrrh, make him spend a frightful night! O blood of the victim, lead him panting! O cemetery broom, bring him to my side!"* '

JAMES A. MONTGOMERY,

Incantation Texts

COMMUNICATION WITH THE DEAD

'It is only within recent times that the attempt to communicate with the dead has been elevated to the dignity of white magic. Here it is necessary to affirm that the phenomena of modern spiritualism are to be distinguished clearly from those of old necromancy. The identity of purpose is apt to connect the methods, but the latter differ genetically. To compare them would be almost equivalent to saying the art of alchemy is similar to *mercantile pursuits because the acquisition of wealth is the end in either case. It needs to be added that occult writers have sometimes sought ambitiously to represent the communication with departed souls by means of ceremonial magic as something much more exalted than mere spiritualism, whereas the very opposite is nearer the truth. Ancient necromancy was barbarous and horrible in Us rites; it is only under the auspices of Eliphas Levi and Pierre Christian that it has been purged and civilized, but in the hands of these elegant magicians it has become simply a process of auto-hallucination, having no scientific consequence whatever. The secret of true evocation belongs to the occult sanctuaries; it is not the process of spiritualism, and still less, so far as may be gleaned, is it that of the magical rituals, nor would the secret at best seem respected by those who possess it, because the higher soul of man transcends evocation, and that which does respond is beneath the initiate.'*

A. E. WAITE,
The Book of Black Magic

SEABURY QUINN

Seabury Grandin Quinn was born in Washington D.C. in 1889. In 1910, he graduated from law school, and was admitted to the District of Columbia Bar. He served in World War I, and after his Army service became editor of a group of trade papers in New York. His first published work was 'The Law of the Movies' (1917), in *The Motion Picture Magazine*, and his first published fictional story was 'Demons of the Night' (1918), in *Detective Story Magazine*. He introduced the occult detective Jules de Grandin as a character in 1925, and continued writing tales about him until 1951. Quinn's stories were incredibly popular, and between the twenties and fifties he appeared in *Weird Tales* magazine more times than both Robert E. Howard and H. P. Lovecraft. His novel *Roads* was also widely read. Quinn died in old age on Christmas Eve.

MARGARET IRWIN

Margaret Emma Faith Irwin was born in London, England in 1889. She attended Clifton High School in Bristol, followed by Oxford University. She began writing books and short stories in the early 1920s, and married children's author and illustrator John Robert Monsell in 1929. Irwin's 'Queen Elizabeth Trilogy' – comprised of *Young Bess* (1944), *Elizabeth, Captive Princess* (1948) and *Elizabeth and the Prince of Spain* (1953) – were esteemed for the accuracy of their historical research (amongst other things, she meticulously researched Elizabethan slang and conversational stylings), and Irwin became a noted authority on the Elizabethan and early Stewart era. Her *The Proud Servant* (1949) was also very popular, and saw readers captivated by the charismatic Earl of Montrose. Of her short fiction, 'The Book' (1930), 'Monsieur Seeks a Wife' (1934), 'The Earlier Service' (1935) and 'The Curate and the Rake' (1935) are examples of some of her more widely anthologised tales. Outside of her fiction, in 1960 Irwin penned a well-regarded biography of Sir Walter Raleigh.

ALEISTER CROWLEY

Aleister Crowley was born in Royal Leamington Spa, England in 1875. Raised by Christian fundamentalist parents, he attended Trinity College at Cambridge University, but left before graduating. Upon leaving the college, he devoted his life to the occult, studying magic, qabalah, alchemy, tarot, and astrology. From 1900 onwards, Crowley travelled extensively, mainly in India and China. In 1904, while in Egypt, he produced one of his most popular works, *The Book of the Law*, and three years later he founded his magical order.

Throughout the rest of his life, Crowley was a prolific writer, producing essays, prose and poetry on a wide range of subjects. In 1913, he published *Magick (Book 4)*, a lengthy examination of his belief system which draws on a vast range of sources and is regarded by many as his *magnum opus*. In his later years, Crowley became addicted to heroin and struggled with bankruptcy. He died in Hastings, England, aged 72. To this day he remains a highly influential figure, both in occult circles and popular culture.

M. P. SHIEL

M. P. Shiel was born in Plymouth, the West Indies in 1865. He studied classics at King's College, London, and upon graduating made the acquaintance of Oscar Wilde and Arthur Machen. After working as a mathematics teacher for two years, Shiel had his first writing success with the 1895 three-part story *Prince Zaleski*. He followed this a year later with his collection *Stones in the Fire* (1896), which includes his best-known fantasy story 'Xelucha'.

By this point a popular and well-read author, Shiel released his popular *The Yellow Danger*, in 1899. Playing on the popular fear of Eastern power and immigration, the novel, along with similar later works such as *The Dragon* (1913), is often credited with the creation of the xenophobic phrase 'the yellow peril'. Shiel also wrote historical romances, such as *The Man Stealers* (1900), before turning to science-fiction with his best-known novel, *The Purple Cloud* (1901). He even found time to pen a series of detective stories as 'Gordon Holmes', which included the novels *By Force of Circumstance* (1910), and *The House of Silence* (1911). Shiel died in 1947, aged 81. His legacy is a mixed one; he is seen as both an exuberant genre-innovator and a somewhat sad, xenophobic figure. His *Times* obituary described him as "a master of fantasy, less widely known than he deserves."

H. P. LOVECRAFT

Howard Phillips Lovecraft was born in 1890 in Rhode Island, USA. Although a sickly boy, Lovecraft began writing at a very young age, quickly developing a deep and abiding interest in science. At just sixteen he was writing a monthly astronomy column for his local newspaper. However, in 1908, Lovecraft suffered a nervous breakdown and failed to get into university, sparking a period of five years in which he all but vanished.

In 1913, Lovecraft was invited to join the UAPA (United Amateur Press Association) – a development which re-invigorated his writing. In 1917, he began to focus on fiction, producing such well-known early stories as 'Dagon' and 'A Reminiscence of Dr. Samuel Johnson'. In 1924, Lovecraft married and moved to New York, but he disliked life there intensely, and struggled to find work. A few years later, penniless and now divorced, he returned to Rhode Island. It was here, during the last decade of his life, that Lovecraft produced the vast majority of his best-known fiction, including 'The Dunwich Horror', 'The Shadow over Innsmouth', 'The Thing on the Doorstep' and arguably his most famous story, 'The Call of Cthulhu'. Having suffered from cancer of the small intestine for more than a year, Lovecraft died in March of 1937.

www.ingramcontent.com/pod-product-compliance
Lightning Source LLC
Chambersburg PA
CBHW030547030726
47495CB00004B/1168